Wesley Chu

WESLEY CHU

The Days of

TAO

The Days of

TAO

WESLEY CHU

SUBTERRANEAN PRESS 2016

First Edition

ISBN
978-1-59606-788-2

Subterranean Press
PO Box 190106
Burton, MI 48519

subterraneanpress.com

The Most Important Man

Nazar Savaryn was good at two things in life: mixing drinks and staying off of people's minds. In his military days, those two skills served him well, because he could drink heavily, and nobody noticed. That all came to an end when he accidentally saved a man he was meant to kill. These days, he still mixed drinks and stayed off of people's minds. However, the man he used to be and the man he was now were complete strangers.

He stared at the oil undulating on the surface of the murky ocean water, his distorted image dancing back at him. There was something wrong with this picture. For a moment, he lost himself in his reflection and wondered where all the years had gone. The person staring back at him looked livelier, thinner and dirtier, just like his youth. That face had none of the dozens of creases and scars time had etched into Nazar's own.

A dead fish and a shredded rubber tire drifted into view, breaking up the reflection and bringing him back to the present. The sounds of waves slopping against the pier and seagulls perched on lamps overhead squawking their ugly song had intruded on his quiet thoughts.

Nazar looked up and scanned the rest of the Port of Piraeus in Athens. There was also something wrong with this picture. For thousands of years, the port had been one of the busiest in the world. It was the heart that pumped commerce throughout the

Mediterranean Sea. Now, it was missing one important thing: ships. There were only a handful moored at the piers. He looked down at his mangled left arm tucked close to his body. Literally one handful. Any more, and he wouldn't be able to count the number on his fingers.

Nazar sucked on the dregs of his hand-rolled cigarette, flicked the butt into the water, and headed back toward the warehouse. He noted the sedan parked just outside the building gates and then swept his gaze once more across the port for signs of anything suspicious. His practiced eye saw movement in eight separate locations: workers walking, lifting, lounging and driving utility vehicles.

The warehouse interior was a far cry from the abandoned and desolate piers. Where the port would be lucky to pull in five fingers' worth of ships a day, this warehouse, and almost every other one here at the docks, was packed to the rafters with supplies. They were getting ready for something big, a large-scale construction project, a new trade route, perhaps a new supply chain. Or something worse.

Nazar found whom he was seeking standing just inside the building's massive double-gates, and moved silently behind him, his hand drifting to the pistol holstered at his waist. The man noticed him approach, and his one-sided conversation with the foremen stopped abruptly.

Nazar filled that beat. "Nine minutes, sir. The delegation will be missing you shortly."

As Anton Boyko's body man for the last fifteen years, it had been his responsibility to be the minister's personal assistant, valet, driver and mixer of old fashioneds. He also kept Anton organized, on-schedule and was tasked with remembering the names of people the minister met.

Without responding, Anton continued to dictate to the three dockworkers standing nearby. Nazar stayed in the background and scanned the premises. On top of his other duties, he was also the minister's first line of defense. He could shoot a man with a pistol one-handed at fifty meters. During his service to the minister, Nazar had never had to draw his weapon. Anton Boyko wasn't the sort of public official or ex-general who one would consider a high-profile target.

Except for that one time.

Anton waved his finger at all the entrances. He had always been quite the finger swordsman. "Security is far too lax here. Double it up." He pointed outside the warehouse to the edge of the property. "Barbwire that fence and establish a no-man's-land all the way up to Leoforos Irinis."

"But Minister," the foreman frowned. "That is a residential area. We do not have the authority—"

"No excuses. Begin today," Anton snapped, and walked away.

Most definitely something worse. Much worse.

Nazar led Anton back to the sedan and opened the door, lighting the minister's cigar before he climbed inside. The cigar smoke filled the interior of the car as the minister grumbled about the many vulnerabilities of the port.

"Where to next?" Anton asked once Nazar got in the driver's side.

"Meeting with your Chinese counterpart at two, one with your senior staff at three, dinner with the Greek president at six, and a massage at nine. Your flight to Tripoli tomorrow morning is scheduled for eight. You also just received a priority message from Russia, informing you that tomorrow is Lucia's birthday."

Anton sat up. "Are you sure that's what it said?"

"Yes, sir." Nazar paused. "I am not familiar with that name. Do you need me to purchase a gift for this person?"

There was renewed urgency in the old man's voice. "Cancel everything. Take me back to the Grand Bretagne immediately. I need to be in the air heading to Moscow within two hours."

Nazar ran through the logistics and political fallout of the sudden change in plans. "Minister, the Greek president is hosting a large gala to honor you—"

"Immediately."

In the fifteen years that Nazar had served the former general and now minister, he had rarely seen the man so affected. "Is everything all right, sir?"

"The next few months will be long, my old friend. Fly your family in to Moscow as well and spend some time with them. It may be a while before you see them again."

That wouldn't take any time at all. Nazar's parents had been dead for sixteen years. He looked in the rearview mirror. Anton's fingers drummed the leather seats. He looked on edge, restless, and preoccupied. Nazar hadn't seen the retired general this way since his military days, though really this civil position was just window-dressing. It was much easier to explain a minister touring foreign lands than a general. The sedan fought through the dense traffic of Leoforos Andrea Siggrou, cutting through the heart of the city. It was taking longer than anticipated and the minister became more agitated by the second.

Nazar took the opportunity to probe Anton about what "Lucia's birthday" meant. The two of them had known each other since the Crimean conflicts, when Nazar first served under the former general. He had saved the man's life, earning him a medal for valor, a promotion to his body man and this mangled arm. Ever since, he had followed Anton as he transitioned out of military life into the political realm. The two of them were now nearly inseparable, and Anton considered Nazar his closest and most important confidant.

As soon as the car pulled in front of the hotel, Anton leaped out and hurried inside. Nazar had to rush after him and nearly missed the elevator to their suite. He stayed silent while Anton ripped off last minute instructions, ordering him to move his staff meeting up to during his flight, to move his own family from Crimea to meet him in Moscow, and, of all things, to make sure his villa at the capital was stocked with American bourbon.

"We might not have many more opportunities to obtain more in the near future."

That last part told Nazar everything he needed to know. The minister had an obsession with many things American: movies, music, basketball, but most of all, he loved Kentucky bourbon. Once in his suite, Anton went to the desk to arrange his documents and classified files, instructing Nazar to pack their things.

Nazar dutifully complied, first going into the servant's room. It took only a few minutes to fill his single briefcase. He scanned the room and then, satisfied, walked out to the main living area.

Anton was still working at the desk. Nazar noticed the brick-sized air-drive plugged into his laptop. The minister finished whatever he was doing, unplugged the air drive, and handed it over to Nazar. "Keep this on your person. I'm going to shower. Make sure we're ready to leave by the time I'm done."

"Yes, sir."

Nazar waited until the minister had gone into the bathroom before pressing his thumb down on the air drive's scanner. He spoke in a clear voice, "Ventidius"—Viqo's greatest achievement—and waited as the voice, password, and thumbprint identification verified his access. A faint green light on the rubber-coated drive appeared for just a brief moment. Satisfied, he patted his pocket for his lighter and awkwardly scooped it into his left hand. His broken fingers grappled the lighter clumsily as he flicked it on. It would have to do.

He gave himself a beat to gather his thoughts and prepare for what he was about to do before walking into the bathroom.

The room was filled with steam from the shower's half-dozen jets blasting Anton's naked body. Nazar could just make out the old man's bare wrinkled ass through the haze. He fanned the air, trying to clear away some of the mist. That was going to be a problem. Still, he had to risk it. Viqo escaping was not an option.

Anton must have somehow felt his presence. He looked behind him and barked out, "what is it?" When Nazar didn't answer, he continued more sternly. "What's gotten into you? Get out of here, and close the blasted door."

Nazar closed the door firmly behind him and approached the showering minister. He cleared his throat. "You remember when I saved you from that assassination attempt?"

"What of it? You're acting very strange, Nazar."

"You got it all backward, sir. I was the assassin. I botched it. The explosive embedded in the binding of the book went off while I was placing it on your desk. Nazar raised his mangled arm. "It earned me this. I appreciate your gratitude though, taking me on as your body man. It afforded other opportunities for those I truly serve. However, it's time I correct that one mistake."

He drew his pistol.

To his credit, Anton Boyko refused to be cowed. "You fuc—"

Nazar fired twice, shattering the shower glass and striking the minister in the stomach. He slammed into the back tiles and slid down to the ground, leaving a streak of red along the wall.

The water continued to rain down on him, mixing with blood and soap.

"After all we've been through," Anton uttered in short, brief gasps. "Why?"

"Savaryn is not my real surname," said Nazar. "It's Sajjadi."

"I..." Anton coughed. "You're a Kurd."

"This is revenge for my family. You killed them during the Night of the Bulshov."

"That's...that's impossible. You've introduced me... I've helped..."

"Hired actors. This has been a long time coming. I've played you for a fool." Nazar pulled the trigger twice more, hitting Anton once through the heart and once more through the head. He holstered his pistol and grabbed a can of hair spray off the counter. He waited as the thick curling steam wrapped around a gaseous sparkling mass rising from Anton's body.

Nazar flicked the lighter several times in his left hand, managing to light a small flame on the fourth try. With his right hand, he shot a jet of fire with the can of hair spray, consuming the shower with the flames until the last of the sparks of light had disappeared. It was hazy enough in here to make it difficult to determine what was steam and what was Quasing, so just to be safe, he continued spraying the flames, blanketing the entire room until the last remnants of steam or Quasing were gone.

"Die, Viqo," he growled.

The lighter and spray can fell from his fingers, and he collapsed to the ground. His chest heaved as long-overdue tears rolled down his face. He thought about his mother and father and his little sister Arryi. He shuddered uncontrollably and wept from the overwhelming relief for having finally avenged them. In the first few years he had served the minister, he had to fight the urge every night to not walk into Anton's bedroom and strangle him in his sleep.

Lastly, he cried for his friend, Anton, the murderer of his family whom he was forced to befriend and serve in order to reach this point, but also a man he had learned to respect and admire. In the end, it became almost as difficult to kill Anton now as it had been to not kill him fifteen years ago. Finally, after twenty minutes, drained from releasing all those deeply-buried emotions, Nazar picked himself off the floor, wiped his wet face, and stared into the mirror. "Get ahold of yourself, man. Now comes the hard part."

He had work to do. He still had to escape. Nazar had to get the black air drive sitting on the desk to Command. That was the most important thing. The information in that drive would not only save lives, but possibly change the course of history. Anton would be missed in a few hours. Every additional minute Nazar spent in Greece was a minute he was in danger.

He hurried back to the living room and grabbed his bag, making sure to put the air drive in the hidden compartment at the bottom. He pulled out his cell phone, took the battery out, and replaced it with another specially-encrypted one he had pulled out from that same hidden compartment. He dialed a number and waited.

"Twenty-four hour wake up service. We wake up to wake you up. Can I help you?"

"Identification: Slot Machine."

"Voice identification matches Nazar Sajjadi. Duress condition verification. Base binary required."

"Binary code zero, zero, zero, one, one, zero, one, one, zero, zero, one, one."

"Cover agent Slot Machine verified with non-duress condition. Transferring. Please hold."

Jazz music began to play.

Nazar placed the phone on the desk and began to clean the room. He threw a match into the trash can and began to add every document, identification and reference to him he could find to feed the flames. For a second, he considered setting the entire suite ablaze, but decided against it. He would need the few hours head-start if he were going to escape.

"Hey, Nazar," a tired voice on the other line finally spoke. "It's been a while since your last report. What's your status?"

Nazar grabbed the phone and put it to his ear. "Wyatt, I need to come in."

Analyst Wyatt Smith put both hands on his headset, removed it, and then placed it on his desk. He stared at his monitor for a good ten-count. He made a slow pivot clockwise in his chair, his gaze sweeping across the room at the mostly empty desks. Pre-dawn was off-hours, after all. Important things rarely happened at this time. Important things happening often required important people to decide they had to happen, and most important people were asleep right now.

Not this time.

Wyatt inhaled. He exhaled. "Holy shit!"

He sent a message to Dawson, the shift supervisor, and then sprinted out of the room, down the narrow concrete hallway of the underground bunker a quarter kilometer below the frozen ground of Greenland. He reached the shift office gasping for air—there wasn't much call for exercise in his line of work—and banged on the door.

"Come in."

"I need someone on the ground in Greece right away." The words came out of his mouth so fast they stumbled over each other. "One of my guys has critical intel. He needs to come in yesterday."

"Slow down, Wyatt. Figure it out. That's your job." Dawson didn't bother looking up from his novel. "Have him send it through encrypted channels. Hell, have him email it."

Wyatt shook his head. "Can't. It's packet-blocked. The data can only transfer through hard-line protocols and requires three-tiered live authentication to access."

"Well, he'll have to figure out how to hoof it here on his own," Dawson replied. "We don't have anyone in Greece. We haven't had anyone around there for two years."

"It's critical matter, sir. An Alert One that is going global in the next five minutes. I forwarded you my notes."

Dawson sighed, dog-eared a page of his book, and then checked his email. There was a lengthy pause between the time the supervisor read the email, dropped his jaw, and spoke. "Oh. Shit. We need to get that man out of there now!"

"Yes, sir, I know." Wyatt did his best to talk slower and less high-pitched. "How can we have no operatives there at all?"

"Well..." A pained look crossed Dawson's face. "There is one, but senior staff made it very, very clear to not activate him at any cost."

"Why not?"

"Because he got a 'D' in Art History."

Cameron

Tell me what you see wrong with this picture.

Cameron Tan stood in front of the large stone carving of a naked one-armed man fighting a naked one-armed three-legged centaur. The plaque in front of it said 'Centaur and Lapith - Loaned from The British Museum in London'. He grunted. "You mean other than the fact the Greeks are getting their own artwork loaned back to them?"

No wonder you flunked Art History.

"Now you really sound like mom. A 'D' is a whole grade away from failing."

Now you sound like your father. But really, what is wrong with this carving?

Cameron tilted his head and gave it a hard look. "Well, the human guy is throwing an overhand right but you can't generate a lot of power from that angle. He's also trying to knee his opponent in between the front legs but I'm pretty sure a centaur's groin is in between the hind legs. Not to mention he's trying to knee the guy while throwing that punch at the same time. While we're at it, his standing support leg is bent, which will only contribute to a loss of power and balance." He pointed at the man's right leg twisted around the centaur's right foreleg. "I have no idea what the heck is going on over there."

I did not expect this conversation to move in this direction but not a bad analysis.

"I feel a C-minus in my near future. Now that I'm looking at it closer, these guys have muscles where muscles don't belong. It's like the ancient Greeks invented the first comic book superheroes."

You should take your grades more seriously. Jill will make your life miserable if you don't get them up.

"Why does it matter? When I graduate in a year, I'm just going to become an agent. Command won't care what my grades are when they hire me. My mom's the Keeper and I'm a host. You're my nepotism by Quasing, Tao."

Your mother will, and you do realize that when you become an agent, she becomes your boss.

"Oof. I didn't think about that."

Cameron continued walking down the row of marble columns, looking at each carving taken down from the metopes and laid out for the exhibit. "Man, these guys really hated centaurs back then."

Cameron was currently wandering the Parthenon in Athens with his study abroad class. Originally, he was supposed to have spent the summer before graduation completing his training as a Prophus operative, but after he received a couple of poor grades at Oxford, his mother felt the need to punish him.

At first, he was crushed. Being a full-status Prophus operative was the only goal he had ever had, from the first moment Tao spoke with him. However, after spending over a month in Greece, he was glad for this punishment. He had lived his childhood as an alien fugitive in the United States and his adolescence guarded in the United Kingdom due to his status as a host and the son of a high-ranking Prophus. This was the first summer he was spending on his own where he had complete freedom. He did not have to worry about what he was or who his parents were.

He loved it.

Well, not totally on his own. Tao was always with him. His eyes wandered to Emily and Seth strolling down the other side of the exhibit. Emily Curran and Seth Fishman were the children of Prophus operatives. Emily's mother reported directly to Jill, while both of Seth's parents worked as analysts with Roen and the IXTF.

The two of them were the first to befriend a shy sixteen-year-old who had just moved from the United States to Glasgow, where many Prophus operatives with families that didn't want to live in Greenland lived. The three of them became close friends, then classmates at Oxford. Now, they were getting ready to graduate and join the family business, although Cameron was the only one who was becoming an operative.

Seth planned on following in his parents' footsteps as an analyst, which was the perfect career choice for him. He was incredibly meticulous and organized, had a way of breaking things down to see the small picture, and was a natural leader of projects, if not people. Seth and Tao were the only reason Cameron ever passed any of his biology and chemistry classes. The sciences were just not in his cards, much to his Quasing's chagrin.

Emily, on the other hand, was the care-free daughter of a Prophus liaison to MI6, and had no idea what she wanted to do with her life. She was planning to work for the Prophus as a chef, medic, chaplain, or something. Her mind changed depending on the season. Right now, she wanted to become a fashion designer for them. Cameron had never realized the Prophus had a need for one until she pointed out the amount of customization and detail that went into tailoring operatives' uniforms.

Both of his friends noticed him looking their way. Emily cheerfully waved with both hands, while Seth rubbed his belly and pretended to put something in his mouth. Cameron checked the time and held up three fingers and mouthed the word 'gyros?' silently. Seth nodded in agreement while Emily pumped two elbows in affirmation.

The study abroad group was a collection of thirty students from all over the world. Cameron had met them only a few weeks ago, but had already become good friends with most of the class, mostly due to his more extroverted friend Emily. He was going to be sad when the summer ended. At least he would have fond memories, which was more than what he could say for most of his childhood summers. He wouldn't admit it to anyone except for Tao, but he was pretty sure this experience was more fulfilling than whatever training his dad had in store for him.

Do not be so sure of that. Roen wanted to teach you how to fly a helicopter.

"Didn't dad crash three helicopters?"

One of them was not his fault.

To Cameron's surprise, his Quasing had very little to say about the Greeks. Cameron had assumed that since Greece was the center of civilization for over a thousand years, that Tao would have a trove of stories to tell.

I spent thousands of years working within the Mesopotamian Empire. By the time the Greeks rose to power, I was burned out and frankly bored. Besides, there was so many of us in that region, if you threw a rock, you were bound to hit a host. That was when I decided to explore other lands.

"Is that why you weren't enthusiastic about coming here this summer?"

Basically. Once you spend three thousand years in the same place, you are pretty much done with it forever.

Cameron totally understood where Tao was coming from. After a few hours here, it was pretty clear that there was only so much ancient ruins a twenty-one year old could handle. As the morning wore on, Cameron and his class became restless and the field trip degenerated into goofing off, gossiping, and taking pictures of each other as opposed to actual relics.

Right now, he was sitting on the grass chatting with Negin Heidari, an Iranian he had a small crush on, and Yang Shi, a wealthy exchange student from China. The Prophus had flagged Yang when they ran the background check on him. It seemed his family's companies had business relationships with Genjix interests. Regardless of Tao's natural bias, Cameron had taken an instant liking to the quiet and stoic heir to a manufacturing conglomerate. The kid loved Shakespeare, basketball, and was a prodigy with the viola.

Negin had come from the opposite corner of the world. Where Yang was a scion from a powerful politically-connected family, Negin hailed from a poor rural village in Iran. Her talent for the written word had been obvious from an early age, and she had earned a scholarship for poetry. Now, whenever she strung words together, regardless of the language, it quieted a room. Cameron also just found her incredibly sincere and a pleasant person to talk to.

At this moment, they were just three students from different parts of the world sitting on a grassy knoll relaxing under the warm rays of the sun while a cool breeze blew in from the Mediterranean. Cameron was telling an admittedly stupid joke about being a few members short of forming a United Nations Security Council. Yang humored him with a chuckle, but Negin openly laughed. Cameron blushed.

You have always had a thing for potential enemy spies.

"She's not a spy, Tao."

She is not a Genjix vessel. That is all we have been able to confirm.

That stung. Of course Tao was referring to Alexandra Mengsk, the Russian-girl-turned-Genjix-Adonis-Vessel who had betrayed him and broken his heart. No, she had not betrayed him, she had played him from the beginning. Cameron hadn't seen or heard from her for over five years, but his mind still wandered to her once in a while. Was she even still alive? How was she doing? Was she now some bad-ass crazy Genjix super-spy? He wouldn't put it past her. Mostly, he never to wanted find out, although a part of him desperately hoped they crossed paths again.

Cut it out. You are making me nauseous.

"Don't you want to know what happened to her?"

Yes, so I can run her through with a sword and burn Tabs up into a crisp.

"And you call me barbaric."

Seth and Emily found him a few minutes later. By now, most of the other students had also congregated on the hill. Professor Eliades, the head of their program, could be heard calling every-one in and corralling the stragglers together.

"Hey guys," Emily said, plopping herself down between Cameron and Negin. She nudged Cameron mischievously. "What are you up to?"

"Hello, my dearest friend," Negin said, putting her arms around Emily's shoulder and hugging her.

Seth knelt down on his other side and whispered in Cameron's ear. "Emily and I have a bet with Annelie and Marilyn. You have four more weeks for us to win a kabob dinner. Don't dis-appoint, Cam."

Cameron's cheeks began to burn.

"Come on, let's lunch." Emily grabbed both Cameron and Negin by the elbow and pulled them to their feet. "Back to campus and then that gyros joint next to the beach?"

"Sounds like a—"

His phone beeped.

Cameron took it out of his bag and checked the message. He frowned at the code in the text. This was unexpected. He casually surveyed his surroundings before slinking off to the side behind a column. Once alone, he took the battery out of the phone and replaced it with another he had stashed in a side pocket of his backpack. He called the number back.

"Twenty-four-hour wake-up service. We wake up to wake you up. Can I help you?"

"Identification Tao. Binary code one, one, zero, zero, one, zero, one, one, zero, zero, zero, one."

"Voice recognition and binary code matches Cameron Tan. Please stand by."

A moment later, another voice clicked over. "Agent Tan, priority activation. You are to rendezvous with a contact at the Perseus's Prick at the corner of Zinonos and Geraniou. Subject: age fifty-one, dark hair, dark suit, 1.8 meters height. Pass phrase..."

Cameron was so surprised he stopped listening. It had been a while since he was last activated. He had difficulties keeping his grades up while going on assignments, so his parents had put the hammer down on new jobs until he improved. His blood raced as the voice on the other line continued providing instructions. He really should be listening, but Tao would catch everything. Right now, he was too stunned to process the information.

"Do you have any questions, Agent Tan?" the voice asked when he was finished.

Cameron said the first thing that came to mind. "Um, does my mom know about this?"

What, really? First job you get in over a year and this is what you say? Baji will never let me live this down.

"The Keeper will be updated on your current status. Unfortunately, you are our only asset on the ground at the moment." The voice on the other line sounded resigned. Cameron could only imagine what Jill was going to do once she found out that they had activated her son without notifying her. Especially while he was in school. The last time this happened, Roen had taken him on a hunt in Norway to raid a Genjix surveillance outpost, or a guy's night out, as he described it, and she went ballistic.

"Are there any resources I can use, a safe house, cache of weapons, contacts, anything? I don't even have a gun."

Seth appeared from around the column. "Come on, Cam, we're taking a picture. Oh." Cameron held up a finger. Seth pointed at the watch on his wrist and disappeared again.

Cameron hunched back over the phone. "I have to go."

"Good luck, Agent Tan."

After the call ended, Cameron stood there for a few seconds to process everything. This would be his first solo mission. In in the past, he had always worked either with his dad or with a team of agents. There was no safety net, and it terrified him. Just a little. Maybe more than just a little.

Well, you have me, although I think we should look at it more like this is my assignment and I have you as an asset. Besides, this is probably a cake job. Command is not going to throw you to the lions first time out on your own.

For a second, a familiar image flashed into Cameron's head of several Christians being thrown into a Roman pit filled with lions.

"Tao!"

Sorry, I could not resist.

"You're not inspiring confidence here."

You can do this, Cameron. You have intelligence, competence, and experience on your side.

"You're right. I can handle this job on my own. I got this," he huffed as he tried to make himself believe those words.

I was referring to me.

"Again, not helping. Did you get everything?"

I did.

"Good because I wasn't paying attention."

I know.

"Great, let's go."

Cameron rejoined the other students just as the class was snapping a group photo. He wasn't sure how he was going to pull this off, since his presence would likely be missed. This specific program had a curfew, and Professor Eliades ran a pretty tight ship. Several students had gotten busted sneaking out at night to go bar hopping.

"I hope I can finish this job quickly and get back before anyone notices."

Get your head right for the upcoming mission. The rest of this is just window dressing. You are a Prophus agent first.

"I'm also a college student."

Emily fell in beside him. "Is everything all right, Cameron? You look distracted."

He leaned into her. "Hey, I have to go check up on something. Can you cover for me?"

"What do you mean you have to go? Go where?"

"Prophus business. It won't take long, I think."

Emily looked around to see if anyone was close by. She hissed, "Cameron, you can't just go. If Eliades notices you're missing, she'll call the cops, or worse, your mom."

"Just tell them I don't feel good and went to bed early."

"Fine, Cam." She threw her arms around him and squeezed. "Be careful." Then she went to grab Seth, and together, they walked to the front of the group. Emily looked back at him one last time before getting the professor's attention and distracting her. Cameron slowed his gait until he was last in the group, and then he ducked into a side alley just as they turned the corner. He took out his phone and pulled up a map.

"All right, Tao, let's get our spy on."

The Mission

Omonia Square was a dump. Cameron kept his head down to avoid eye contact as he passed through crowds of vagrants, drug dealers and thugs lounging in the streets. Sketchy storefronts, crowded alleys and heaps of trash littered the landscape. The lights emanating from burning oil drums dotting the blocks cast long shadows that seem to dance against the walls. The air of danger seemed to linger everywhere.

Cameron subconsciously brushed his hand to his back pocket to make sure his wallet was still there. "Are you sure we're in the right place?"

Were you expecting your contact to meet you at the Four Seasons?

"That would have been nice."

You have gotten soft over the last few years, Cameron. Ever since you moved to the United Kingdom, life has been too easy. You have forgotten what it is like to live life on the edge.

Cameron grunted. "I lived my entire childhood as a fugitive, Tao. A kid doesn't forget stuff like that. It's etched into my brain for life."

He proceeded across a narrow side street, past a shady-looking corner bathhouse and down a set of broken stairs into a bar called Perseus's Prick. Cameron felt the hairs on his neck rise as he entered a long, thin room that had just enough space for a bar counter on one side and a row of small tables on the other.

The bar was crowded, but surprisingly quiet. The patrons here were older, grizzled, and every single one of them eyed him up and down, wondering what a fish-out-of-water like him was doing here. He must not have invited much thought, because after a cursory glance, most just showed their backs and promptly forgot he existed. There was a constant buzz of low chatter and whispers, as if everyone here was muttering at the same time.

Cameron squeezed into a spot at the counter at one end of the bar. It was the only seat available, and the guy next to him reluctantly offered the room only after Cameron nudged him aside with an elbow. He ordered a glass of ouzo and took a sip, doing his best to not make a face. Personally, he thought the traditional Greek drink tasted like awful licorice, but he had learned from his dad to always embrace local cuisine. Cameron sat at the counter for the next ten minutes, pretending to sip and stare at his drink while he surveyed the rest of the bar.

"Who's the contact?"

Man, fifties, suit.

Cameron swirled the ouzo in its glass. "That's all we got? Half the guys in this bar fit that description."

So find the right one. Come on, get moving.

Cameron picked up his drink and began scoping the joint, his eyes darting left and right as he passed, hoping to not attract unwanted attention while making contact with the right man in his fifties.

Wearing a suit.

"Thanks."

So far, he had nothing. Most patrons were huddled in small groups, glaring at him warily if he got too close. All who were alone looked as if they preferred it that way. Nobody looked like he wanted to talk to him. Maybe it was just the way he looked.

Taking that a little personally, no?

"How the hell are we supposed to find the right guy?"

I have been too lax with your education. You are one of the most skilled fighters I have ever trained but you suck as a secret agent. There is a lot more to being an operative than just combat. In fact, fighting will be the smallest part of your work.

"I'm sorry, Tao, but secret agent wasn't a major at university."

No one told you to become a History major. In fact, your parents, all three of us, told you to study something useful. You might as well study Music Theory.

"God, now you sound like mom. Those who do not learn history are doomed—"

Why do you need to study history at all when you have me? I lived through just about everything.

"I wanted an easy 'A'." Cameron replied, crestfallen.

Yet you got a 'D' last semester.

"Art is hard!"

Cameron finished canvasing the front half of the bar and went down a small set of stairs to a lower level. It was even darker and smokier here than the front. A dozen pairs of eyes zeroed in on him and he felt tingling down the back of his neck as he walked by several clusters of people. He saw the glint of a knife and heard the scrape of a chair being pushed back. He tensed.

Relax. It is nothing. You acting tense is making everyone else around you tense.

"What? You're saying this is my fault?"

Undoubtedly. This is where a theater degree would have come in handy. Being a good actor is integral to being a good secret agent. I found our contact anyway. He is in the back right corner.

"How do you know?

See that suit he is wearing? It is wrinkled.

"So? Half the guys in this dump are wearing wrinkled suits."
*Look more carefully. Most of the suits here have seen better days.
Now look at his: modern cut, tailored, high quality wool. Look at his
face. That is the look of someone staring too intently at his drink, but
his attention is focused on everyone else in the room. See how he reacts,
just a little, when someone gets close?*

In this low light, Cameron couldn't tell if the guy was wearing
a bathrobe or a suit so he just had to take Tao's word for it. He made
his way to the back corner and sat down opposite the contact. The
man, early fifties by the look of it, had alert eyes and carried a tinge
of nerves about him. His right hand caressed a glass of wine while
his left was tucked under the table. A handgun perhaps?

"Tao, what's the pass phrase?"

*You need to learn to listen better and not blank out all the time.
Here.*

Cameron annunciated each word carefully. "Always remember that you are unique."

"Just like everyone else," the man replied. He squinted and
sized Cameron up. "You are younger than I expected. A host?"

Cameron nodded. "Well, Command is a little short on operatives in the region so they had to dig me up from auxiliary."

He stuck his hand out. "Nazar Sajjadi."

Cameron shook it. "Cameron Tan."

He is not a host.

"Ooh, I outrank him."

Nazar raised an eyebrow. "Tan, Tan. By chance are you…"

"Her pride and joy."

The older man grimaced. "Now I'm not sure if I should be
taking a bullet for you or the other way around."

"How about neither of us take a bullet." Cameron countered.
"What's the job?"

"I have time-sensitive information that needs to be safe-guarded. Your mission is to escort me to Greenland."

Cameron managed to keep his face neutral, but inwardly, he groaned. He had hoped this was a short and easy assignment, and that he could make it back to his study abroad program. "How much heat is on you?" he asked. "We can't just book a flight?"

"I murdered the Russian Quartermaster General. I assume the entire country is looking for me right about now."

Cameron drew a blank. "Well then, uh…"

"Unfortunately, I have a distinguishing feature that makes me easy to identify." Nazar raised his left arm and put it on the table. "The Genjix and the local authorities will definitely be tracking the airports, transit systems and roads by now." The older man reached forward and gripped Cameron's hands tightly. "We have to hurry. Lucia's birthday is tomorrow. An attack is imminent!"

Cameron frowned. "Wait, what's imminent? Who's Lucia?"

"It's a code, a signal." Nazar leaned forward and spoke in a low voice. "Listen, boy, war is about to break out. If we don't get out of here right now, we'll be behind enemy lines soon."

Cameron's stomach twisted tighter into knots as Nazar briefed him. Since humanity had discovered the existence of the Quasing some sixteen years ago, the countries of the world had taken sides with either the Prophus or the Genjix. For the past five years, after the IXTF, the Interpol Extraterrestrial Task Force, had allied with the Prophus, the two factions had been on a collision course toward open conflict, with both sides daring the other to make the first move. The rest of the world had gotten used to their posturing after a while, and most believed it was simply shaping up to becoming another Cold War. Now, if what Nazar said was true, they were on the eve of World War III.

And it would start any day now.

"Lucia's birthday." The words barely escaped his lips. He felt like the weight of the whole world was on his shoulders.

It is apt, if not imaginative. Nazar is right. We have to get him out of here at all costs. Tonight.

"Who is Lucia and what's the deal with her birthday?

Lucia was Erwin Rommel's wife. Her birthday marked the D-Day invasion.

"Uh, so are you saying the actual attack is commencing tomorrow?" Cameron asked. "Like an all-out global blitzkrieg?"

Nazar shrugged. "I don't know for sure. All I know is that Lucia's birthday is a catalyst to war. It will set everything else in motion. When Anton received the code, he ordered us to head directly back to Moscow, which means it's happening soon. My life isn't what's important." He finished his drink and pulled out a brief-case. "In here is an air drive that has detailed maps and information for the Genjix's supply lines for the entire European theater."

What? Ask him if it includes tooth-to-nail ratio.

"What's tooth—"

It is a military term. You would know what that is if you had enrolled in Sandhurst like I told you to. Just ask.

Nazar nodded when Cameron brought it up. "Projected for the first six months of the theater, including warehouses, facto-ries, depots, and projected inventories."

This information is vital to Prophus efforts. We have to do what-ever it takes to get this into Command's hands.

"That's why we have to leave as soon as possible," Nazar stressed. "The information in here could determine the outcome of the war."

"When do we leave?" asked Cameron.

Nazar held up his drink. "As soon as I finish this. We need to head to the town of Loutsa on the western coast and rendezvous with a Prophus extraction team. They will take us to Italy, and then the IXTF will fly us to Greenland."

Cameron's mind raced. Things were moving faster than he anticipated. "I…I need to tie up some loose ends."

I know what you want to do. I do not recommend it. The smart thing to do is leave right now with Nazar. The sooner, the better. We will have higher chance of success if we travel with a small group.

"Tao, I have to bring Seth and Emily with us. They are my best friends, and they're Prophus. They'll never survive behind enemy lines."

Nazar checked his watch and tapped the table impatiently. "We don't have much time. I don't know what happens once Lucia's birthday hits."

"An hour is all I need," Cameron replied. "Please."

This is a mistake, Cameron.

"Maybe, Tao, and I may come to regret going back for them but I know I'll definitely regret it if I leave them behind."

"Very well." Nazar shook his head and sighed. "I hope you realize what is at stake. I am at the hotel Ira's Hearth, room 262. Find me when you are ready."

"Thank you." Cameron stood up and offered a hand. "I'll be back soon. I promise."

Nazar shook it. "Hurry back. The fate of the war to come may rest in your hands, son of the Keeper."

The Plan

Cameron left Perseus's Prick moving at a brisk jog. Any faster, and he would likely have attracted the wrong sort of attention. Besides, this wasn't the right neighborhood to run headfirst without looking where one was going. It could have been a trick of his eyes, but for some reason, everything seemed darker now, more ominous, as if the shadows were closing in and threats were coming at him from all directions.

You are feeling nerves. This is nothing you cannot handle. You are young in age but long in experience. Empty your mind and focus on the job.

Cameron imagined he was about to fight and suppressed his nerves. His training kicked in and he relaxed, the tightness in his chest loosening as he slowed his breathing. Time slowed and he felt aware and sensitive to his surroundings. Movements around him became a complex game of chess. It was up to Cameron to analyze and decide how to react. He was back in control.

Good. Get to work.

Tao had said Cameron had the potential to be one of the greatest hosts—the Prophus's version of the Genjix's Adonis Vessel—ever since Cameron was a child. Adonis was a term both he and Tao detested. While the skill comparison was apt, he was completely different from his Genjix counterparts.

The Adonis Vessels were bred in the Genjix eugenics program to be lethal instruments serving their Holy Ones. Cameron's
link with Tao went much deeper. Tao had joined Cameron when
Cameron was five years old, and after decades of training in Tai
Chi and being together, the two had developed the most symbiotic relationship ever seen between Quasing and human.

To be fair, whenever he got a big head about it, Jill would
remind him that Baji—Jill's Quasing—had thought that about
Sonya, her previous host, as well. It seemed every Quasing at one
point in time had believed their new protégé could be special, so
Cameron took those high praises with a grain of salt.

*Actually, no one ever thought Roen was going to be the greatest
host. He surpasses my expectations even to this day.*

Cameron weaved through the busy crowds, keeping his head
low and watching for anything suspicious. The city was on edge,
but that had always been the case on the border countries. He had
just never noticed until now. Perhaps it was here all along, but he
was just too self-involved to notice. For years, everyone predicted
the eventual outbreak of war between the Prophus-backed and
the Genjix-controlled countries. Now it was actually happening.

The very thought of a global war terrified him.

*We need to discuss this mission's parameters and prioritize our goals
and risks. You have a big heart like your father. That is commendable,
but it will get you killed one day.*

"It didn't kill dad."

Technically, it did. How else do you think you got me?

"Well, I'm going to start calling him a zombie from now on then."

He is starting to move as slowly as one.

"Ouch."

*I know you want to take your friends with you, but the stakes are
high. Let them work through the Prophus extraction protocols.*

Cameron shook his head. "It'll take at least thirty-six hours to mount an extraction. You heard Nazar. It'll be too late. Greece may be a contested region by then. The university is fifteen minutes away. I'm already here on the ground. I can fetch them and be back to Nazar in no time."

This is the wrong choice.

"Duly noted. Look, Seth's family invites my folks over for Hanukah every year. Emily's mom comes to all our Thanksgiving dinners. They're practically family. How can I face their parents ever again if I know something bad is happening, and I just abandon them? This is my wrong choice to make and I'll face the consequences."

No, Cameron. When you make the wrong choice this time, it affects me, Nazar, and all of the Prophus.

For a moment, Cameron's inner calm collapsed and panic once again seized his chest. Could this guy really be the linchpin for the war, and was he being a dumb kid screwing everything up because he didn't want to leave his friends behind? Was he just selfish and stupid? At that moment, he nearly turned around and headed back to Nazar. However, the instant that urge reached his brain, he knew he could never live with himself if he followed through. He gritted his teeth and moved on.

Cameron reached the University of Athens campus twenty minutes later. It was early evening and the rust in the sky was washing over the landscape. He found most of the students hanging out in the rec room of their dormitory. Some watched television, others played pool, and a group was nesting on the couches gossiping. Two students were hovering over a table in the corner pro-actively working on their finals project.

Six of his classmates were couples at the moment, although that number fluctuated by the week. Cameron waved at Emily, who was currently too preoccupied cuddling with Chris, the son of an American professional golfer, to notice him.

Chris was the blond good-looking guy most of the girls had crushes on. He also was the most boisterous and usually the center of attention. He was a nice enough guy, but Cameron could tell he had lived very few hard days in his life. Personally, Cameron thought Emily could do better but he didn't dwell on who she dated too much.

Cameron involuntarily snuck a peek at Negin. She was sitting in between Seth and Annelie, the Swedish graduate student. That made him feel a little better. Everyone knew he liked her, but that meant little unless he actually asked her out. He was too shy to make a move, so he lived in fear of seeing her with another guy.

One day, your puberty will end and I will sing praises to the Quasing gods.

"You blobs have gods?"

Not exactly. The Eternal Sea on Quasar tends to consider itself a living god of sorts although the interpretation is not exact.

"Hey Cameron," Annelie called out. "When are we going to start on our project? We're not even halfway done."

Annelie had blue hair and was the most studious in class. Unlike Cameron, who tended to rely on Tao to finish things at the very last second, she liked to get things done ahead of schedule. Most of the partnered teams hadn't even started working on their projects yet.

"Tomorrow," he lied. "Promise."

She nodded, but didn't look like she believed him. He ignored her squint and pursed lips.

Now that you are here, what are you going to tell them?

"I don't know. Any suggestions?"

This one is all you. I recommend pulling Emily and Seth aside and stealing off into the night, but what do I know? I am just an ancient and wise alien who is never wrong.

That sounded like a good place to start. Trying to act as discreet as possible, Cameron tapped his two friends on the shoulders and asked them to meet him outside for a smoke. This was their agreed upon signal in case of emergencies.

"What's going on?" Emily asked as she handed out cigarettes to each of them. All three lit their sticks and pretended to take a drag. None of them actually smoked and were making a pretty poor display of it. Seth actually inhaled and began to cough.

"We need to leave the country," Cameron began. "According to one of our agents, the Genjix is starting a war any day now. Greece is about to become a battlefront."

Emily, the future medic, chef, clothing designer, didn't take that news well. "Oh no! What do we do? I'll start packing. Can I call my mom?"

Seth was staring off into the distance. Cameron had seen that look on his face hundreds of times. The guy always thought before he spoke, and spoke before he acted. He was processing this information, and was already running a mental checklist and considering his options. Like a good future analyst, he began to ask the right questions. "How good is the intel? How much time do we have? Are the Prophus sending anyone to pick us up?"

Cameron started with the easy answer. He grabbed Emily by the shoulder. "I have a plan to get us out. Sort of." He turned to Seth. "Intel comes from a well-placed source. Not much, and there's supposed to be an extraction team meeting us in a village called...called..."

Loutsa.

Cameron repeated that information.

A long pause passed between them. Finally, Emily asked the question on all their minds. "What about the others? Do we tell them what's going on?"

"We shouldn't," Seth said firmly.

"How can we not?" said Emily.

They both looked at Cameron.

"Tao says the three of us should just go right now," Cameron replied, downtrodden.

Emily crossed her arms. "Well, I think we should invite them to come with us. Give them a chance to escape before it's too late."

This should not be a democracy, Cameron.

Cameron glanced at his two friends, and then thought about what Tao said. In his head, he knew that leaving now, with just the four of them including Nazar, was the smart choice. However, in his heart, he knew it would haunt him. After a few agonizing seconds, he reluctantly made his decision.

"Pack your things. Meet downstairs in fifteen minutes. Tell no one."

Seth nodded. "See you soon."

Emily scowled and stormed off.

That was the right call. Sometimes, it is impossible to make everyone happy.

Cameron hurried after Seth and went upstairs to his dorm room. He didn't have much to pack. It had been ingrained in him as a child fugitive to live minimally. These days, he practically survived out of a duffel bag. He stared at the small collection of relics and souvenirs he had slowly accumulated during his time here. Those would have to stay. Most of his clothes too. He just needed bare necessities, his few personal valuables, and weapons.

He definitely needed weapons.

Unfortunately, the only thing that could remotely serve in a fight was a dull steak knife he had smuggled from the cafeteria to cut fruit. It would have to do. He threw on a hoodie, hid the knife in his right sleeve, and slung the duffel bag over his shoulder. He checked the room one last time, the pile of things he was leaving behind already forgotten. Attachment to physical things was a luxury in his world.

You need to head back to Nazar. It has already been an hour. You need to learn to pad your numbers better.

"Not now, Tao."

Cameron hurried back downstairs and waited outside for the others. Neither of his friends had arrived yet. A few students passing by looked at him curiously. Cameron turned his back to them and pretended to be preoccupied with his phone. The fewer questions he had to answer, the better.

Seth came out a few minutes later wearing his backpack. "We have a problem."

"What is it?"

"Emily and Chris are fighting in the rec room."

Cameron sighed. "Oh man."

He and Seth hurried back into the building. They could hear Emily and Chris's voice all the way down the hallway.

Chris looked over at Cameron when he walked into the rec room. "Hey Sun, what crazy crap are you feeding my girlfriend? She says the world is ending or something, and you're making her leave." Sun was Cameron's assumed surname at the university.

Girlfriend? They have been dating for two days.

They were attracting more curious eyes by the second, which was the last thing Cameron wanted. Pretty soon, they had everyone in the room's attention.

"Where are you three going?" Annelie asked. "What about our project, Cameron?"

"Were you going to leave without saying goodbye?" Negin said, seemingly a little hurt.

Cameron felt flush. He looked over at Seth and Emily. "Can I talk to you guys for a second?" He pulled them outside the rec room. "What did you tell Chris?" he hissed. "Why?"

Emily looked on the brink of tears. "I...I told him we had to leave because you said something bad was happening. I'm sorry. I had to say goodbye."

"Well, we made a commotion and now people are asking questions. We can't just leave them hanging," said Seth. "We have to tell them something or they'll probably run to Eliades or maybe even the police if we just disappear on them."

"Just tell them the truth," Emily said.

"Might as well warn them now that they know something is up," Seth added.

"Fine, I'll keep it vague," Cameron said, exasperated. "I'll say I came across some bad news and thought it was a good idea to head home early." He wouldn't admit it but a small part of him was relieved he was forced to warn the other students. It felt like the right thing to do. Maybe it'll save lives.

At the very least do not reveal the source of the conflict. These people do not need to know who and what you are. Promise me that.

"Hold up," he said, tugging on Emily's arm. "Tao wants to make sure we don't reveal that we're Prophus."

Her mouth dropped. "Oh god no, were you actually going to tell them? I thought you were just going to lie and say something like a terrorist threat or Mt. Vesuvius erupting."

Mt. Vesuvius is in Italy.

Cameron corrected her.

She shot him a glare. "You hush, smartass."

"I agree with Emily," Seth frowned. "Admitting you're inhabited by an alien to our fellow students is a nutty idea."

Cameron felt a little foolish. Apparently, he trusted these people more than his friends did, which disturbed him, because he was the one who's supposed to be the future secret agent. They returned to the rec room. The crowd had grown and Cameron was now very conscious of everyone waiting for him to say something.

He cleared his throat. "Um…"

"Tao, what should I say?"

How about "Come with me if you want to live."

"Now you're just making fun of me."

I am, because you are wasting time. Speed this up. Time is of the essence.

"Hey guys." He drew a blank. "I, um, I came across some news. Something bad is about to happen. Seth, Emily, and I are leaving the country before it's too late…"

Clever. Original. Cryptic. Well done.

He was met with silence, some confused looks, and a couple chuckles. Everyone seemed to be waiting for him to say something else.

"…and I think you should all get out of here too."

Chris snorted. "Come on, Sun, where did you get the drugs and why aren't you sharing?"

His snicker was soon joined by Chris's best friend Nick, a Canadian who often bragged about being some expert computer hacker. Cameron didn't know much about the guy. The two had hardly exchanged more than ten words since they arrived. Half of the students began to titter while the other half turned back to whatever tasks he interrupted them from. It was obvious no one took him seriously.

He was almost thankful when Marilyn Ndunguru, a Tanzanian student, began to grill him. "What do you think is going to happen, Mr. Sun? How did you come by this information?" Marilyn had this charming way of addressing everyone as Mr. and Ms. that Cameron found adorable.

Cameron stuttered a few lame responses, none of which were remotely believable. For a second, Emily's Mt. Vesuvius alibi sounded awfully tempting, but these guys weren't dummies. He wouldn't fool anyone. Besides, he was an awful liar. Tao often lamented how bad he was at it, citing it as an Achilles heel in his future career as a secret agent.

It's true. Lying, charm, and a well-fitting suit are the traits that distinguish James Bond from every other asshole with a gun.

"I don't think I even own a suit."

You do not own the other two either.

In the end, he just accidentally spit out the truth. "I think the Genjix bloc countries are going to attack the Prophus ones any day now."

Damn it! I thought you would have learned by now. This is such a tactical error it makes me question why I wasted sixteen years training you. Can you even grasp what a colossal mistake this is?

Surrett Kapoor perked up and looked over from in front of the television. "Those alien factions have been on the edge of war for years. What makes you think anything is going to happen now?"

"I…I just do," Cameron replied lamely.

Surrett was actually good friends with Cameron. Like Chris, he was the son of a semi-celebrity, a Bollywood actress. Unlike Chris, who told everyone on the first day about his golfer father, no one knew about Surrett's mother for weeks until it accidentally slipped out one day. Other than that, he was just a nice guy to hang out with.

Chris's father is ranked just outside the PGA top one hundred. He is as much a celebrity as the punter on a football team. Second of all, if you want everyone to drop everything and follow you purely on your words, those words better be convincing.

Cameron coughed and tried to muster the right words. Coming up blank, he resorted to pleading. "I'm sorry but I can't get into details but you have to believe me. It's for your own safety."

That was not convincing at all. In fact, you are making it worse.

By now, he had reached the limit of most of his friends' short attention spans and had lost the crowd. Some looked at him with concern, others just shrugged and found something better to do. Eyes that were focused on him moments before were now wandering back to the television, or the people next to them, or wherever they were focused previously.

Cameron heard words like 'crazy' and 'high' and 'weird' tossed around. These were insults and descriptions hurled at him all his life. Different. Off. Not normal. He was all these things to the rest of the world. Even the people in the study abroad program, students whom he considered friends, thought he was something other than one of them. His ears burned and he turned to leave.

You did all you could. It is time to go.

A few people pushed past him into the room. A few seconds later, others followed, rushing past him. The rec room all of a sudden filled up.

Emily tapped Cameron's shoulder and pointed at the growing crowd gathered in front of the television. Curious, the three moved closer to get a better view. Nick grabbed the remote and turned up the volume.

A news anchor had interrupted the regularly scheduled broadcast and was giving a special report. Several of the students turned to Cameron. He and Seth were the only ones who spoke a little Greek. Cameron had told his class he had learned the language, but it was actually all Tao. Seth actually studied Greek for three months before coming here. Usually, his classmates leaned on them for help ordering food.

Negin nudged him. "What are they saying, Cameron?"

Translating through Tao, Cameron repeated what the anchor said. "...is being enacted at 2200 hours. All citizens are ordered to stay in their homes. General Topopulus, chief of the Hellenic National Defense General Staff, has declared martial law. Anyone caught outside after curfew will be harshly dealt with. A travel ban is imposed on the following countries." Cameron stopped. The next words came out a near whisper. "The Greek government has declared its allegiance with the Genjix bloc."

It is too late. We are now in enemy territory.

None Left Behind

It was dead quiet in the rec room. Some students huddled together, others stared out the window, most talked uncertainly amongst themselves. Still others were glued to the television, their laptops and phones, hungry for more news about the events unfolding.

The news websites and social networks were ablaze. Some called it a Greek alliance with the Genjix countries, others a coup. Where was Prime Minister Tsikiras? Where were members of the ministry? What did this mean for the country and its people?

More unconfirmed reports began to filter in through various channels. Large ships were spotted by the Hellenic Coast Guard moving into the Aegean Sea. Tanagra Air Base reported a series of loud explosions. The Koufovouno Army Base on the far eastern edge of the country had gone completely dark. The entire power grid for the city of Komotini had gone down.

Together, the individual pieces of news began to paint an unsettling picture. This was a planned and coordinated coup. It wasn't long before the words 'under attack' and 'civil war' began to leak into the conversations.

Then someone said the magic words. "The Internet is down!"

"I can't call home!" someone wailed.

All hell broke loose. Everyone began frantically checking text messages and typing on their laptops. People were running around, praying and hugging each other as if it was the end of the world.

Cameron sat in a chair off to the side, rubbing his temples with his fingertips. Athens was on lockdown. If he had just listened to Nazar, they may have gotten out into the countryside in time. Now it was too late to escape.

"I really messed up, Tao. I'm sorry."

Worry about that later. Right now, we need to plan our next move.

"I should have listened to you. I just…"

Stop apologizing and stop being so hard on yourself. That is my job. Focus on the situation. I will scold you later after we are safe. Right now, the priority is to smuggle Nazar out of the country. The longer he remains in Greece, the more likely the Genjix will find him.

A large group of students was huddled together whispering loudly. Several looked his way. Chris broke off from them and approached him. "You knew all about this, didn't you, Sun?" His tone was more accusatory than a question.

You cannot trust anyone. Tread carefully. You think you know these people after spending a summer with them but you do not.

"I knew something was happening, but not what exactly," he replied.

Surrett, who was looking back and forth between the television and Cameron, frowned. "Are you one of the Genjix, Cameron?"

He shook his head.

"A Prophus then?"

Cameron hesitated, just for a split second, but that pause was enough to give him away. He grudgingly nodded. "I have contacts within the Prophus."

"But you're still leaving, aren't you?" said Negin, her face painted with worry. "You have a way out of this country?"

Cameron nodded.

"You have contacts within the Prophus, and they're going to evacuate you out of Greece?" Surrett sounded incredulous.

"Can you take us with you?" Negin asked.

Absolutely not.

The room filled with bickering about what to do next. Most seemed intent on staying and waiting out the crisis. A few were clamoring to join him, while an equal number, if not more, were calling him heartless for abandoning them here.

Negin and Surrett were to his right, begging him to take them. Chris and Nick were to his left, demanding him to do the same. All of them were basically declaring that their lives were in his hands, and that he was sentencing them to death otherwise.

"Both Canada and United States are on the travel ban list," Nick said. "We're trapped here. If you have a way out, take us with you. Otherwise, our death will be on your hands."

"The United Kingdom is on the list too," Negin pleaded. "I have to get back to Cambridge. I am the first person in my village to attend university."

"You're all crazy," Marilyn said. "This will blow over soon. I'm staying right here."

The chatter grew louder and the students became more aggressive until, slowly, Cameron found himself backed into a corner.

I am not opposed to you just fighting your way past them and making a break for the door.

"I can't beat them up!"

You cannot possibly bring your entire class out of the country.

"I'm sorry, I can't help," Cameron said, miserably, shaking his head over and over again. However, slowly, the crowd wore him down. It was too difficult for him to look them in the eye and repeatedly tell them no when they thought he was their only chance of survival. The guilt was overwhelming. He felt as if he was personally sentencing all of them to die. Eventually, their looks of hope and fear broke his resolve.

Do not cave in to them, Cameron.

"Fine," He said, raising his hands. "I can take a few. Just a couple though." By this time, it was so loud in here no one heard him. He reached out and pulled Seth and Emily closer. "Seth, go to Eliades's office and get the van keys. Emily, you talk louder. Help me corral these guys."

Seth nodded and ran off. Emily looked as if she might punch him.

"That's not what I meant," he said hastily.

She threw him a scowl and then climbed on top of a chair. She projected over the noise. "All right, shut up. If you want to come with us, be ready in ten minutes. Otherwise, you're on your own."

That got through to a few students. Several rushed out of the rec room, presumably to pack, or hide under their beds, or whatever. At this point, Cameron had reached the limits of his patience. He was getting out of here, with or without them.

Emily checked her watch and tapped it. "Ten minutes starting now."

Seth returned a few seconds later. "Professor Eliades's office door is locked. I don't know where she is."

"So break the window then," Cameron said.

Seth blanched. "I can't break a window."

Remember, they are civilians.

Cameron tried really hard not to roll his eyes. "Just throw something at it. It's fun. Go, hurry."

At the ten-minute mark, only a few students who said they were coming had returned to the rec room. Annelie and Yang ran up to them. "Hey, Cameron," Yang said. "We're going to get our stuff. Don't leave without us, okay?"

Cameron exchanged glances with Emily. "Uh, sure." He watched them walk away casually and turned to her. "What were they doing all this time?"

Emily shrugged. "Probably deciding if they wanted to join us. In any case, they better get their asses moving."

Cameron decided to give his classmates a few more minutes. At the fifteen-minute mark, he gave them another extension. Twenty minutes later, they were still waiting. By now, Tao was yelling in his head to leave. Emily had also lost her patience and was doing so in his ear. Seth, thankfully, had volunteered to fetch the stragglers. Finally, after thirty minutes, Chris, the last person, strolled into the rec room.

Cameron stared at the full-sized hard-shell luggage the American rolled into the room. Then he noticed Yang's viola case, Negin's backpack full of books, Annelie's telescope, and the full-sized desktop strapped to Nick's back. Cameron felt a vein pop in his neck.

Like I said, civilians.

He pointed at Surrett's three carry-ons. "What do you have in there?"

"Clothes. I sweat a lot."

Cameron felt his hands contort into claws. He held up two fingers. "Two bags. That's it." He pointed at Nick's desktop. "That is not coming with us." He glared at Yang. "Neither is the viola."

Yang crossed his arms. "This is a Bartolomeo. I'd rather die than part with it."

"That can be easily arranged," Cameron snapped.

Easy there.

"Everyone's pissing me off, Tao!"

Like herding pubescent cats.

Emily got in between them. "Guys, we're not going on vacation. Pack light and make sure it's something you can run in."

Everyone grumbled, but most began to shed stuff. All except for Chris. He flatly refused to unpack his gigantic luggage case. "I need everything inside." He made a flexing motion. "Besides, I'm strong like bull. I may end up needing to help some of you weaklings along."

Once they were all ready to go, Cameron surveyed the ragtag group. The final tally was ten classmates joining him. He prayed he wasn't leading them to their deaths.

Maybe Tao was right.

Is there ever any doubt? Add you and Nazar makes twelve. How the hell will you shepherd twelve people all the way across a country under martial law? This is a complete disaster.

Cameron sighed. He was risking his and Nazar's life, not to mention the critical data in the air drive to try to bring these people to safety. It was a stupid move, but he wouldn't be able to live with himself otherwise. This was the risk he had to assume to avoid a guilty conscience.

"Let's go." He opened the door and waved this sad-looking bunch out of the building.

Ira's Hearth

"What are you doing?" Annelie gasped as he unlocked the school van's door. "You're stealing school property."

"They have bigger things to worry about than missing this jalopy." Cameron slid into the driver's seat and started the ignition. "Come on."

Everyone else climbed in, but the Swede hesitated. "This feels like a mistake. Stealing is a crime."

"It's not too late to change your mind," he said. "But we have to go now."

In the distance, plumes of smoke were rising from downtown Athens. The light from scattered red glows of fire merged with the rust of the setting sun. The unmistakable sound of gunfire, pops and cracks, intermittently punctured the air.

Annelie shook her head. "I can't do this. I'm staying."

He nodded. "Take care of yourself, Annelie."

A chorus of goodbyes followed.

Now we are down to eleven.

Cameron adjusted the rear-view mirror and looked back at his new wards huddled in three rows of seats as the van rumbled down the asphalt road and turned onto Kesariani Street heading toward the heart of the city. The group was mostly silent. They drove by more signs of civil unrest with each passing kilometer:

burning cars, shattered windows, protesting mobs, blockades. In the distance, he could hear the faint rat-tat-tat of gunfire.

The whispers grew in the van grew louder. Someone began to cry.

You have to put them at ease. Let them know things are under control, that things will be all right.

"How can I tell them that, Tao? I can't even convince myself. This should feel like any other mission, but it doesn't. It's freaking me out."

You are feeling the weight of being responsible for others. You have never had to look out for others before, except for that one time.

Except for that one time was their code for referring to anything remotely related to Alexandra. It was one of those things that he would have to put up with for the rest of his life.

Surrett slid up to the front seat next to him. "Cameron, are we heading to your Prophus people?"

"We're heading into the city. Is that wise?" Negin said, coming up from behind him and putting a hand on his shoulder.

"We deserve to know the truth, Sun," Chris piped in. "If you're screwing with us, and we get in trouble for being truant, we're going to have problems."

Cameron tried to keep his cool. "We're going to a hotel to pick someone up, and then we're going out of town."

"What guy?"

"What's the name of the hotel?"

He gritted his teeth, not taking his eyes off the road. "Just... hang on. Let me concentrate."

It was hard enough to drive in these conditions without being interrogating. Dusk had settled over the city. The streets were poorly lit and littered with zooming motorcyclists and bicyclists, not to mention everyone drove like they owned the road. The traffic became thicker as they approached the down-town area, until soon, they had slowed to a crawl. Sirens and car horns blared into air, joining the awful chorus of bumper-to-bumper traffic.

Cameron checked the time. This was taking way too long. Maybe allowing his friends to come was a bad idea. Was he going to be too late getting back to Nazar? Were the Genjix or the police going to catch him before Cameron could reach him? Did Cameron just sentence a guy to die?

"Tao, help me."

Continue on foot. Pull over on the left into the Church of St. George. It should be only a two kilometer walk to Ira's Hearth.

Cameron pulled into the church's parking lot. He got out and beckoned for the others to follow. "We'll go the rest of the way on foot."

More protests followed.

"How far is the walk?" Nick whined.

"Are we coming back for our stuff?" Chris asked.

Just tell them yes.

"I think so." Cameron had no idea.

That is not a yes.

Chris opened the back trunk and pulled out his luggage. "Doesn't sound like you know, Sun. I'm going to bring mine with me just in case."

There was a chorus of agreements and Cameron watched helplessly as the rest of the group followed Chris's lead. Pretty soon, the eleven of them were walking down a narrow Athens street with everyone carrying their luggage. He looked back at the sullen group trudging behind him. Most did not want to abandon the van. He was their de facto leader, but already, there was dissension among the ranks.

A foreboding vibe hung in the air as they made the trek toward Ira's Hearth, yet none of his wards exhibited any sense of urgency. He wished he had a pistol. He wished his father was here. Hell, he wished he had something better to defend himself with right now than this stupid fruit knife.

To his relief, they reached Ira's Hearth without any incidents. Chris's large boxy monstrosity lost a battle against the uneven brick street and sent a wheel spinning off. Now, he was dragging the thing behind him with one corner constantly scraping against the ground. That damn thing was not going to last the night.

The entrance to Ira's Hearth was off a main street in a side alley down a set of steep stairs. Between the barred windows, broken stones, and with half the display lights on, it looked nothing like a hotel. Cameron checked the address twice, and then stared at the wooden sign next to the entrance long and hard before deciding this had to be the right place.

Seth stared dubiously at the crooked sign. "We going dungeon crawling, mate? This place looks seedy."

The group followed him down the stairs, their luggage thunking down each step. They entered a narrow worn-down lobby where a bored clerk sat behind a desk. The man, hair covering almost all of his body except for his head, barely looked up. "By the hour. No women allowed. That one is down the street. No more than four to a room."

Cameron ignored him, and led the group upstairs and down a narrow hallway under the haze of blue and red lights and walls decorated with framed pictures of nude men and small statues of Greek gods in compromising positions.

"What kind of hotel is this?" Seth asked.

"I don't know want to know."

He found Room 262 and knocked on the door.

"Who is it?" Nazar's voice came from the other side.

Cameron repeated the pass phrase, and the door swung open. Nazar's mouth fell open when he saw the gaggle of young people behind Cameron, and reluctantly allowed them into his room. The eleven of them in total could hardly fit.

Nazar surveyed the group and then looked down at Yang's viola case. "You said you had to tie up loose ends, not bring the entire marching band."

"It's a viola," Yang replied. "They don't use violas in marching bands."

"Who is this?" Surrett asked.

"Who are you?" Nazar shot back.

I hear sirens.

Cameron raised his voice and his hands. "Everybody just calm down."

Their next door neighbor thumped the wall and shouted "Shut the fuck up!"

Negin tugged on his sleeve. "Is it too late to go back to the dorm?"

Order disintegrated once more.

Sirens! There are police outside this building.

Cameron noticed the blue flashes of light just outside the window and put a finger to his mouth, shushing everyone. Everyone quieted, and shouts from downstairs soon bled through the floors and walls. The voices grew louder and were followed by the thump, thump of footsteps walking up the stairs. There was a sharp banging of doors, and more shouts and curses followed. The pattern repeated, each time growing a little louder.

"We're too late," Nazar hissed. "They found me."

"We don't know that. It could be anything. Quick, in here." Cameron pushed everyone into the bathroom. He turned to Nazar. "Try to get rid of them."

They left their luggage on the floor on the opposite side of the bed and then crammed into the tiny room. They were just able to fit everyone in after a fair amount of configuring. Seth and Nick stood on the toilet, Surrett sat on the sink, and the rest huddled in the tub. Cameron closed the door until there was just a sliver left open so he could get a direct view of the front door. He slipped the knife into his hand.

There was an aggressive knock on the door. Nazar walked up to it, looked back at Cameron, and then answered in Greek. His thick Ukrainian accent was replaced by rough nasally voice. "Who is it?"

"This is the police," the voice yelled. "Open up!"

"What the fuck do you want? I'm busy here," Nazar replied.

"Open up or you will be arrested for resisting arrest."

Nazar looked over at Cameron again and gave him a what-do-I-do shrug. Cameron pointed at the door and willed his body to relax as he cleared his mind. Fighting the Genjix was one thing, fighting law enforcement was a whole other issue. That was walking was a fine line. The police had to be treated carefully. They weren't the enemy, but he still had to do what had to be done.

The door opened the chain lock's length. Nazar muttered through the opening. There was a harsh back and forth, and then the door flew open with a loud crack. Nazar stumbled backward onto the bed as two policemen barged in and piled on top of him.

Four men. Armed with batons. One at the door has pistol drawn. Go non-lethal.

Cameron took a breath to visualize the scene, and then he emptied his mind and burst out of bathroom. Time slowed as he reached the first policeman at the door. He grabbed the arm of the gun-hand, raised it to avoid accidental discharge, twisted and then spun, using his momentum as leverage for a throw. In real-time, the policeman barely had a second to cry in pain as his arm jerked at an awkward angle before his body slammed into the far wall.

The second policeman turned to face Cameron and was rewarded with a punch to the face and a quick slice of the dull fruit knife to the back of his hand that made him drop his baton. Cameron caught the baton with his left hand and, using both weapons, slashed horizontally, scissoring the man at the knee and at the side of the head. He crumpled to the ground.

The two remaining policemen on top of Nazar froze, batons quivering in their hands. Nazar, laying on his side with his hands behind his back, just stared mouth-opened. The silence was broken when the hotel attendant at the door decided to book it down the hallway.

I forgot to take him into consideration. Here, say this.

"Let him go. Drop your weapons. Take your friends and leave," Cameron said in awful, broken Greek.

The two men looked at each other, then at their two comrades, and scampered toward the two unconscious policemen to drag them out of the room. As they passed him, he reached out and grabbed the cords to their radios and yanked them off. Cameron picked up the pistol the first policeman had dropped and tucked it into his back waistband.

"Leave your magazines," he shouted after them in English. "Hey, hey!" It was too late. The men had already turned the corner and fled down the stairs.

Worry about the rounds later.

Cameron helped Nazar to his feet. "We have to go."

The bathroom door creaked open and his friends filed out. They all stared at him, terrified, as if he had turned into some sort of monster.

"What the hell was that?" Nick asked. His face was white as a sheet.

"You attacked police," Negin said softly. When Cameron offered her a hand, she pulled back.

Cameron's stomach twisted into knots but he held it inside. "We have to go."

Fortunately, Seth and Emily were there to help. Emily guided the other students while Seth pulled him aside. "Everyone's spooked right now." He pushed Cameron out the door. "Give us just a second to calm them down. Go on ahead."

We do not have time. The two policemen will have radioed for backup once they reached their vehicles. Get Nazar downstairs now. If the police return, be ready to leave your friends.

Cameron looked at his still-terrified friends and, feeling numb, dragged Nazar out the door. The looks on their faces killed him. Just when he finally thought he had found people who accepted him, this happened, and again, he was the freak, the guy who didn't belong.

Listen, Cameron, you are special, and being so does not make you a freak. You are no more different than a math genius or a musical prodigy. You have very unique skills and must own your greatness.

"I just thought it would be different with these guys."

Cameron and Nazar headed downstairs to the lobby and looked out the narrow front window. Unfortunately, all he could see were the front steps up to the ground level. He went to a mirror hanging on the wall and struck it, causing long spidery cracks to appear from the center of impact. He pried out a long glass shard and motioned for Nazar to stay put. Holding the mirror at an angle, he opened the door and crept up the stairs. No sooner did the tip of the mirror reach ground level, then a gunshot shattered it into fragments. He stumbled back, nearly losing his balance as an explosion of shards burst near his face.

A dozen worried thoughts entered Cameron's mind. What if there was no other exit? Had he just trapped all of them in here? How did the police even find them?

Problem solve your predicament and prioritize. Gather everyone up and locate another exit. There has to be a back door, or perhaps a window onto the roof. Most importantly, Cameron, stay calm. Take control.

Tao's strong and soothing words were exactly what he needed. A switch flipped in his head and again, time slowed. He hurried back downstairs. By now, his friends were gathered in the lobby.

"There you are," Emily let out a sigh of relief.

"Hey, Sun," Nick began. "Some of us were thinking—"

"This is not the time," Cameron said, cutting him off. He pulled Seth and Emily close. "Help me keep the group together."

He didn't wait for them to acknowledge him as he pushed his way toward the back of the hotel. A few moments later, after passing through the kitchen and a storage area into the utility room, he found a set of cellar doors opening outward. Cameron motioned for everyone trailing behind to wait as he unhinged the lock. He reached for his newly-acquired pistol.

No. Do not draw your sidearm. You are tactically disadvantaged. Better to let them take you alive than try to fight your way out.

Cameron didn't much like that, but Tao was right. He took a deep breath and pushed the cellar doors open, half expecting to face flashlights and gun muzzles. Fortunately, the only thing that hit him was the terrible stench of garbage. He stuck his head out of the opening like a gopher and swiveled it left and right. He was in the middle of a long narrow alley. To his right was an overflowing dumpster and to his left, a busy street.

That may be Menandrou or Tsaldari. Head that way, and make your way back east toward the van.

Cameron motioned for the others to wait downstairs. "Wait until I check topside."

He stepped outside and ran to the end of the alley. There was a policeman standing with his back to him a few meters away from the entrance. Cameron glanced both ways, making sure the coast was clear, and then leaped out, putting one hand on the policeman's mouth and one below an armpit. He dragged the man back inside the alley, lifted him up, and slammed him on the cobblestone. He quickly rummaged through the man's possessions and took his pistol and spare magazines.

"Hey guys, the coast is..." Cameron looked behind him and saw the entire group standing there, staring at him. "...clear."

Their faces were a mixture of horror and shock and fear. He took a step toward them and all of them—save for Seth and Emily—took a step back.

Chris stepped in front of the group as if protecting them from him. "Listen, Sun, a couple of us have been talking. You assaulted a bunch of cops. We didn't sign up for this. I can't have a criminal record. My dad will kill me. We want to go back to the campus."

"This whole country isn't safe," Cameron said.

"I was safe until I followed you. Give us the van keys." Chris held out his hand. "I think if we make it back to our ride, we can make it back to the university. If Eliades tries to bust us for stealing the van, I'm throwing you under the bus for that one."

"Chris..." Cameron said.

Let them go. You cannot help those who do not wish to be helped. Besides, the smaller the group, the better.

Cameron bit his lips, and then handed the keys over. "Good luck. Stay off the main roads if you can."

Chris nodded. "I don't know what the hell you're up to, Sun, but good luck to you too." He glanced back behind him. "Who's coming with me?"

To Cameron's surprise, only Nick and two others stepped forward. The rest stayed put. Chris looked over at Emily and held out his hand. Emily didn't miss a beat as she crossed her arms and stayed standing next to Cameron. At that very moment, he adored his best friend.

With a shrug, Chris, still dragging that giant hard-shell luggage with the bottom scraping against the ground, led Nick and the two girls in the other direction. Before they turned the corner, Cameron heard Chris ask Nick if he knew how to drive stick.

Nick did not.

And then there were six. Seven with Nazar.

Cameron was losing them one by one. Some kind of leader he turned out to be. Every friend that abandoned him felt like a personal failure. There was a shout from around the corner. He turned to the rest of the group. "Anyone else want to leave or have something to say?" When no one responded, he nodded. "Okay." Cameron looked down the street and pointed. "Let's go."

Actually...

He pointed the other direction. "That way."

Escape

On Tao's advice, Cameron herded everyone west of Ira's Hearth at a full sprint. The group tried valiantly to maintain the hard pace he kept while lugging their backpacks, duffel bags, briefcases, and carry-ons. It would have been comical if the situation weren't so dire. After all, he had just beaten up three police officers.

By now, evening had set on Athens. It was a moonless sky, and the faded lights from the street lamps struggled to beat back the night. Shadows and dark shapes leaped out from alleys, behind corners and garbage bins.

Cameron didn't call for a break until they reached an alley that led between two buildings to a parking lot behind them. The others, unused to this exertion and overstimulated from anxiety, collapsed, exhausted. The first thing Cameron did after they had a moment to catch their breath was force everyone to unload all of their excess baggage.

It was like pulling teeth, but one by one, he was able to reduce each person to one small pack. He forced Negin to leave all of her books, which were a bunch of romance novels. He made Surrett ditch his video game system. Even Emily had a stack of fashion magazines stowed away that she claimed she had forgotten about having in her bag. Yang was the only one who steadfastly refused to leave his viola. Cameron let that one slide. For now.

"Tao, what's next?"

Head northwest. Stay off the main streets. Once you near the edge of town, procure a vehicle and take it to the countryside.

"I don't know if these guys can make it that far on foot."

Traveling by car in the city is dangerous. You are bound to get stopped or stuck in traffic. The roads are always awful during coups.

A roar coming from the main street began to crescendo. Cameron signaled for the others to stay put and then crept back down the alley. A rumble of footsteps heralded a mob passing through the nearby intersection, chanting something he couldn't quite make out. Down the street, glass windows from storefronts shattered. Projectiles were hurled through the air, striking cars and exploding against buildings.

This is bad. Avoid this mess at all costs. It may be a protest, it may be a riot. In either case, it will attract the police and the military. Once this chaos engulfs you, you will lose people. Circle around and then double back.

Cameron hurried back and roused the group, pushing them away from the burgeoning riot. He didn't know how long they ran, just south then west and then north, following parallel to Leoforos Athinon, down a narrow street to a dilapidated part of town. Everywhere Cameron looked, the chaos spread. Rioters and political activists chanted and threw bottles and rocks. Seedy individuals and thugs eyed them, sensing easy prey. At one point, a long convoy of tanks and jeeps passed nearby.

A gang of youths attacked them near the intersection of Kristali and Sikionos. Cameron made short work of them. Another unruly group harassed them near Thivon. This time, he wasn't putting up with any of this nonsense. Flashing his pistol got them past without incident.

The crowds became sparser the further they got from the city center. Run-down industrial centers gave way to neighborhoods and eventually, all the roads narrowed to no more than a car-width wide. Cameron wasn't taking any chances though. He skirted from narrow streets to alleyways to dark gravelly roads and eventually to narrow winding paths where the cars couldn't pass.

They finally reached a neighborhood at the edge of town bordering the foothills some two hours later. Cameron ordered a stop and took stock of his beleaguered group. Most looked dead on their feet, even though according to the maps, they had hardly traveled six kilometers from Ira's Hearth. Emily was helping Surrett stay upright. Negin was holding up Yang. Seth looked like a valet carrying everyone's bags.

"We can't keep this up," he muttered. "We need to hole up and rest for a bit."

A way out of town would be better. Once you get to the forested areas to the north, you should be safe.

Cameron led the group behind an apartment building to a narrow path flanked by two cement walls. He climbed over one of the walls and found a small yard and deck area on the ground level. He checked the garage and found no car parked. He went to one of the shuttered windows and peeked inside. It was dark. Cameron went back to the yard and gently nudged the metal gate open, wincing as a high-pitched squeal cut into the air. He beckoned everyone in. His friends collapsed, exhausted and thankful to be off their feet.

It is the leader's responsibility to check the wellbeing of his people.

Cameron took this advice to heart. He stopped and spoke with everyone individually, checking for injuries. He thought he sounded like an insincere jackass when he tried to lift their spirits and felt like his words fell on deaf ears. Most of them didn't react except to nod. Yang was busy checking on his viola, Negin and

Emily could barely keep their eyes open, and Surrett and Seth were already passed out.

It comes with experience. You will get better at it with time.

Cameron looked over them like a worried mother. He knelt over the slumping Seth and pinched his nose. "Stop snoring, buddy. You'll give our location away."

Seth snorted awake. "Hey Cam, everything okay?"

"Yeah," Cameron said. "I wanted thank you for rounding everyone up back at the university and then later at Ira's Hearth. I can't do this without you and Emily."

"We got your back, bro." Seth yawned and was soon snoring softly again.

Emily crept by and sat down next to him. She pushed his head with a finger until it lolled at a different angle. Seth's nose stopped whistling. She flexed her finger and winked. "It's all about how you tap the melon. Don't worry, oh captain, my captain, I'll make sure the rookie here doesn't give away our position."

A rare smile came to Cameron's face and he squeezed her hand. He got up and moved down to the person at the end of the line. "Nazar. I'm going to scout ahead. Watch over them."

"Actually, I've been meaning to speak with you." The older man stood up pulled him aside. "I don't know who these people are, but they are slowing us down. Are you sure it's wise to bring them with us?" He patted this briefcase hanging close to his body. "You know what is at stake."

I will not tell you what to say, but consider your options carefully. History will not judge you poorly for making the right decision.

Cameron wanted so badly to yell at Nazar and Tao and call them heartless bastards, but he knew both were right. Cameron was the bleeding-hearted fool. He looked back at his friends huddled against the wall, and then back at the man whom Cameron was entrusted with protecting. There were only bad choices. However, as far as he was concerned, making a choice to leave anyone behind was no choice at all.

"We leave no one behind," he said, determined. "This is the last we will speak of this."

Nazar shrugged. "As you wish, Cameron Tan, son of the Keeper."

Cameron looked up at the building and walls encircling the yard. "Stay here unless you are forced to move. I'll be back in an hour."

Nazar drew his pistol. "If something bad happens, I'll fire three shots into the air, two and then one. Got it?"

Cameron nodded, and then hoisted himself onto the wall. He tightrope-walked to the side of the garage and climbed the metal grating protecting the windows until he reached the roof of the three-story building. He stood on the corner of the roof and scanned the horizon.

To the west was the airport, which would most definitely have a heavy military presence. To the south was the sea and the ports, and the way back east was the heart of the city. That left only one direction to take.

"What street is that below?"

Filis. If you take it all the way north, you will hit the foothills.

"One of these days, Tao, you have to teach me how you do that."

Do what?

"Every time we go anywhere, you have the map of the entire region memorized. What's the trick?"

It is easy. The trick is I am much smarter than you. See that strange light source north near that road? That should be Attiki Odos, the main highway heading out of the city. Check it out.

Cameron jumped the gap to the next building over and rolled out of the steep drop, relying on the free-running skills Jill had taught him what felt like a lifetime ago. He scaled another wall, crossed rooves, bounded over obstacles, and hurdled over alleyways. He continued north, avoiding the street level unless he had no other choice.

Now that he traveled by himself, he moved quickly. It didn't take long for him to reach the last building before Attiki Odos, a five-story apartment complex near the top of a hill. He crept to the edge of the roof overlooking the highway and peered over the side. It took a few seconds for his eyes to adjust from the darkness to the blinding white lights, but after a closer inspection, he realized that he was looking at a military blockade.

The roads are no longer an option.

"How are we going to get out of the city then?

Your only option is the foothills into the forest.

"We'll never make it on foot."

Find a ride then. You will need an all-wheel drive vehicle.

Cameron frowned. "Most of the vehicles here are tiny cars or hulking vans."

You passed by a construction yard on your way here. There might be something there.

Cameron backtracked the way he came, again using the rooftops as cover. It was so much calmer here than down on the ground level, peaceful even. It also brought back memories of the long free-run training sessions he used to have with his mother. He missed those times. Those days were long gone. It had been weeks since they last spoke and months since he last saw her. Jill was now consumed with being the Keeper and leading the Prophus. All he was doing was having a good time in Greece. He needed to be a better son and a better Prophus.

Yes you do. Roen would appreciate a call sometimes too.

"Dad's always traveling and dealing with the IXTF. I don't blame him, though, with mom always working those crazy hours. That and he hates Greenland with a passion."

It wasn't easy to have such a busy family. Everyone was fighting the Genjix their own way. As far back as he could remember, his dad was always away. Even if he did prove his conspiracy theories true, it was something Mom rightfully held over Dad's head.

Cameron found the construction yard a few blocks away from where he had left his friends. He scaled the barbed wired fence and began to poke around. There was a skeleton of a building, possibly a warehouse or a mid-rise. He found a cement mixer and a crane, and what looked like a baby bulldozer. None of these would work, though the cement mixer had possibilities as a last resort. He ventured deeper to the back of the yard to where raw materials were stored: stacks of concrete, bags of sand, pallets of lumber and mounds of dirt. There, he found an old truck with a wooden bed.

A tour around the truck told him it had been used recently. A quick break-in through the driver's side window told him he could jump-start it. With a little luck, there would be enough diesel in it to get them out of the city. Cameron was about to get to work when he stopped.

Two shots.

Then he heard it. The third gunshot.

Cameron scrambled out of the cab of the truck and booked it. He threw caution to the wind as he climbed over the nearest fence, sloppily cutting himself against the barbed wire lining the top. He ran as hard as he could, barreling over a stranger who tried to obstruct his way. The man may have been trying to rob him. Lucky for him Cameron was in a hurry.

It was pitch-black now; there wasn't a street lamp in sight. All of the buildings here looked exactly alike as well. Cameron wouldn't know where to go if Tao hadn't led him back to the right place. He bounded over the wall and rushed to the back, only to barge into a confrontation between Nazar, wildly waving his pistol, and an older rotund man with a receding hairline wielding a shotgun. The rest of the group was huddled behind Nazar. The rotund man was shouting and speaking so fast no one could understand him. He probably lived there, because he was wearing a bathrobe.

Three meters distance. Weight is on his hind leg. Left-handed. Go low before he notices you. Be sure to pull the shotgun toward you instead of away, or you risk an errant shot striking your friends.

Cameron was about to put Tao's plan into action and take out the man's legs when he noticed two other figures standing behind him. It was a woman and a little girl. Cameron stopped dead in his tracks. Instead of attacking, he raised his hands and spoke as calmly as he could.

"Parakaló, parakaló."

Slowly and carefully, he waved at Nazar to put his pistol down. Cameron then moved in front of the shotgun. He repeated the phrase.

"Parakaló, parakaló."

Please, please. It was one of the few Greek words he could pronounce reliably without Tao's help.

"Tao, tell him we come in peace."

Cameron, through Tao, told the man that he and his friends meant no harm and that they were running from the chaos in the city. He told them they meant to rest here for just a bit before going on their way. The man kept the shotgun trained on him, spoke loudly and rapidly, and repeatedly waved his shotgun at the entire group. It wasn't until his wife put a hand on his shoulder that he finally lowered it.

The woman whispered gently to the man, and then stepped in front of him. She spoke in a soft voice, pointed inside her house, and then at the gate, and then she tapped her chest twice on the heart. For a second, she gave Cameron hope. It sounded like she was offering shelter and a place to rest. Perhaps maybe even a meal. He was starving, having skipped lunch and dinner today.

She says she is bringing her family inside and wants you assholes to leave. If we stay around, she will shoot you herself.

"Wow, I read that one all wrong."

Keeping his hands up and his body in between the shotgun and his friends, Cameron slowly retreated to the back gate. He shielded them until his friends picked up their belongings, and was the last to get shoved out into the alley. The gate slid shut with a metallic *thunk* followed by an almost equally loud *thunk* of the lock clicking.

Cameron didn't realize he was holding his breath until they were all outside. The rest of the group, unused to being threatened at gunpoint, was shaken up. He put a hand on Nazar's shoulder. "Thank you for taking care of them."

The older man nodded. "These kids are worthless, but they're young and have many more years to lose than me."

That was brave and humanitarian of you. Do not ever, ever do that again. It was too much of an unnecessary risk. I did not put all this knowledge and training into you just to have some trigger-happy jerk plug you with a rusty lever-action shotgun.

Cameron was about to snap back at Tao when the rumble of a convoy passing nearby cut their conversation short. He checked the time; they had approximately four more hours before dawn. Once the light came, they would be forced to hole up somewhere else. The further away they got from the city, the better.

He kept Nazar close to him and put Seth in the far back, trusting him to keep an eye on the others. Cameron felt like a mother duck leading his ducklings across streets. The group moved in a single file, snaking around the back alleyways and creeping across yards and hiding in bushes. Sometimes, they would be forced to wait behind cover as more vehicles—all police and military—drove by.

It took them another half-hour before they finally reached the construction yard. They found a loose gate and pried it just wide enough for everyone to fit through. After a few failed attempts, he was able to get the truck started. He checked the fuel gauge; they had a little under a half-tank of diesel.

Make your way to the foothills.

"Got it. What's the quickest route?"

The fastest path anywhere is a straight line. You are in a dump truck. Run that gate over and pave your own way.

The Villa

They were fortunate to reach the edge of the residential area and get into the forest without encountering a patrol. They were even more fortunate that Cameron didn't plow into a house or a tree or, later on, drive off a cliff. The dump truck was every bit as unwieldy as it looked.

Cameron had to drive the truck through moderately forested areas that were thick enough to provide cover yet still light enough for a truck to drive through. Some of the foliage was so dense Cameron couldn't see past the nose of the truck. Add that to the uneven terrain, filled with rocky crags and sudden steep drops, and the trip into the countryside became the slowest, most nerve-wracking and terrifying drive Cameron had ever had to make at ten kilometers per hour. It was like watching a potential slow-motion train wreck every thirty seconds.

Negin and Surrett were sandwiched in the cab with him while Nazar, Yang, Seth, and Emily stayed in the back. Cameron wasn't sure which seat was worse. On one hand, the ones in the back were able to lie down and stretch out. On the other, being on a truck bed while hitting some of these bumps couldn't be fun. At least the ones in the back got to sleep. He had not planned for an all-nighter when he had woken up that morning.

Surrett at one point had offered to drive, but Cameron insisted he was fine. It wasn't that he didn't trust Surrett with the task…

actually, it was exactly that. He didn't trust anyone with the job. He was the leader, and he already felt like he was barely holding things together.

This is not how leadership works.

"You always tell me that the leader has to be responsible for his people's wellbeing."

Yes, but that does not mean the leader has to do everything himself. Learn to delegate.

"Cameron?" Negin asked, her voice quiet.

"Yes?"

"You move like a whirlwind. Where did you learn to dance in such a way?"

"And those things you can do," Surrett added, "like hot-wiring the truck and shooting guns. You are comfortable with violence, it is obvious."

"Are you one of them?" asked Negin.

One of them, as in no longer one of us. Were Negin and Surrett going to treat him different now if they found out the truth? No, they already did. He could see it in their reactions. When he moved close to them, they tensed or sometimes flinched, as if fearing he was a dangerous animal. Should he tell them the truth?

Be careful what you say.

He simply nodded.

"You're one of the Prophus," Surrett frowned. "Do you have... one of the aliens? A Quasing?"

Cameron didn't answer. He kept his eyes focused on the space a few meters in front of the truck. That was as far as he could see without lights: shadows, tints of darkness, and outlines of shapes.

Finally, he nodded again. "I do."

The conversation died after that admission. Cameron wasn't sure for how long, but it lasted from just before the last crest of the hill, then down the other side to the dried riverbed and halfway up the next.

Negin was the first to break the silence. "What's it like? Does it hurt?"

He shook his head. "Only when he yells at me or hurts my feelings."

Oh poor you.

"What's your alien's name?" Surrett asked.

"It's not important," Cameron replied.

"Are there Prophus in India?" he asked.

Cameron shrugged. "Probably. The Prophus and IXTF are all over the world. Why?"

His friend looked out the window. "It's not a secret that India can't stay neutral forever. I just hope my country chooses the right side."

Stop the truck.

"What is it, Tao?"

Just do it and then get out.

Cameron dutifully complied, pulling the truck to a stop on the slight incline of the hill. He got out, walked ahead several meters in front of it, and stared into the dark abyss.

"What's going on?" Negin called out.

I recognize this place. You see that mountain in front?

"Not really." Cameron pointed in front of him. "There?"

To the right of that. Up about a quarter ways should be a villa on top of a rolling hill.

Surrett stuck his head out of the window. "What are you doing, Cameron? Are you conversing with your alien?"

Cameron ignored them. "I don't see anything, Tao. How do you know?"

Like I said, I lived here for thousands of years, and the stars change little over time.

"Who lives there now?"

No one. It belongs to the old Keeper, Meredith's family. Thousands of years ago, it was the Keeper's residence, better known as a Temple of the Oracle.

"Holy crap, she was *the* Oracle?"

There were a few competing oracles sects. The Keeper's never made it mainstream.

An image flashed into Cameron's head. All of a sudden, it was day again, and he saw a winding dirt path cut into the side of a mountain leading to a small gray temple with two rows of burning urns leading to the entrance. An old, bent, sun-parched woman stood at the doorway, flanked by four young girls. All wore white robes that draped down to their ankles. The old woman's eyes were bound by a white strip of cloth.

"Is it intact now, or is it a bunch of ruins? More importantly, does it have four walls and a roof?"

Even better. She built a summer home next to it a few hundred years later after the oracle business dried up. Even soothsayers love modern amenities. The former temple became the stables, then later storage. The Keeper was never one for sentiment.

"Will she care if we use it? She hates your guts."

Probably, but oh well.

"Oh well indeed."

"What is it, Cameron?" Negin asked again. He felt her hand on his shoulder. "Are you all right?"

He pointed into the darkness at where he thought Tao said the villa was. "I think we've found a place to stay for the night."

She frowned. "I can barely see your hand, let alone where you're pointing."

He clasped her wrist and gently directed it to the right direction "Trust me."

"I do, Cameron."

He felt a slight tingling. He also heard a noise coming from inside his head, something like a groan or a grunt.

Using the stars and Tao's memory, they eventually found the dirt path that Tao had shown him. Unfortunately, just as they turned onto the road, they ran out of diesel and had to go the rest of the way on foot. By the time they reached their destination, the birds were starting to chirp, which meant the sun wasn't be far behind.

Calling it a villa was a bit of a stretch. It was more like a two-story shack, with three bedrooms and four other small rooms that once served different functions. The kitchen, or what was left of it, was its own separate building in the back yard. It was also dusty, seemingly having not been lived in for years. However, it was a roof over their heads and beds to sleep in, so no one complained.

Nazar and the girls each got a room, and the guys shared the largest. Cameron decided that even though it seemed they were in a remote area, someone should keep watch. He settled down to take the first shift.

Negin shook her head. "You've been going hard, Cam. We're going to need you for the days to come. Why don't I take the first watch?"

It would be nice. You need the rest badly.

Cameron wasn't comfortable trusting anyone to keep watch, but he was so exhausted, he accepted her offer. He passed out as soon as his head hit the mattress and slept soundly for two hours, according to Tao. Then his worried mind woke him up and he went to check up on Negin. He found her on the front porch curled up in a chair, completely passed out.

Civilians. Go figure.

He went back into the villa and grabbed what was left of a throw from one of the old couches and covered her up to her neck. Negin shifted in her sleep and maybe murmured thank you, then was once again oblivious to the world.

Cameron sat down on the stone railing and leaned against the corner of the building. His vantage gave him a clear view of the valley below, and there was now enough daylight to see the path they had taken all the way up from the road. In the distance, he could just make out Athens, or at least see the smoke rising from it. There were a dozen dark gray stacks that reached up and out into the sky.

The city had to be in the grips of chaos. He wondered how many people were hurt or injured, how many fewer people were seeing the sun rise. Was this happening elsewhere? Everywhere?

Yang came by few minutes later. "I heard you leave the bedroom. I couldn't sleep, so I came to keep you company."

"I came to check up on Negin," Cameron replied.

Yang grinned at the sleeping girl and then sat on the railing opposite of Cameron. He leaned his back against the front column and stared out into the valley and beyond. "It looks bad, doesn't it?"

Cameron nodded.

"We'd have been stuck in there if it wasn't for you. You got us out in time."

Cameron said nothing. He picked up a handful of rocks from the ground and began to toss them down the hill one by one. He thought about the students who were still trapped there: Annelie, Marilyn, Chris, Nick, and the others, the ones he had failed to convince to come with him. What would happen to them?

That is unfair, Cameron. You did all you could. More than what honor and duty would ask.

"My duty was to get Nazar out. Seems I'm failing that too."
Wait until his funeral before you declare your mission a failure. He is still alive as far as I know.

Yang followed Cameron's lead and picked up his own handful of rocks. "I…I wanted to thank you for letting me bring my viola. I know you didn't want to."

Cameron grunted. "You're the one without any clothing. I'm sure a clean pair of underwear looks good right now."

"Only if it's cotton, so I can wipe down the viola with it."

Cameron bounced a pebble off of Yang's chest. "You're obsessed, dude."

"We all have our vices." Yang bounced one off Cameron's leg.

It became a game of close-distance stoning as the two pelted each other with pebbles. It continued until Cameron miscalculated and hit Yang's glasses. Yang took off his glasses and scowled at the scratch. Cameron made an apologetic shrug and dropped the remaining rocks in his hand.

Yang put his glasses back on and looked out over the valley again. "Why don't you get some rest? I'll take watch. We need you at your best. Besides, you're grumpy when you're sleep-deprived." He looked over at Negin. "Don't worry, I'll stay up."

Cameron swung his legs off the railing. He had to start trusting people one of these days. "All right. Thanks."

He headed back into the villa, but instead of going upstairs to the bedroom, went to the back yard. He sat down on the bench, took out his phone, and held it up in the air. The government must still be blocking the wireless network. He took out the battery and replaced it with the encrypted spare he kept in his back pocket. Cameron took a long deep breath and slowly exhaled. He called the wake-up service and authenticated himself, and then he had them transfer his call.

Jill's voice came sharp and forceful. "Cameron, about time you reported in. Where have you been? Are you in Italy by now? Be careful. That entire country is a damn humanitarian crisis. I can't believe Dawson activated you. I gave everyone explicit directions that you were to focus on your studies. When I get my hands on him, he's going to wish I sent him to a Siberian outpost. Anyway, what's your status?"

"Hi, mom." Pause. "I'm still in Greece."

Jill exploded. She started shouting so loud Cameron had to pull the phone away from his ear.

"Tao, have you noticed mom getting more short-tempered over the past few years?"

I used to think Meredith was just loud and mean, but now I think it comes with the job.

"Maybe it's you, Tao. You're the common thread in both cases."

Apt observation, Mr. Tan.

It took Jill about two minutes of motherly ranting and raging before she got it out of her system. Then she went into full Keeper solutioning mode. "Where are you? Are you injured? What resources are available? Are you being followed? Is our agent with you?"

Tell her where we are vacationing. Baji will get a kick out of that.

Cameron told her everything that had happened from the moment he was activated. It took Jill all of five minutes to put together an escape plan. To be honest, the relief Cameron felt for his mom taking over was more than a little shameful. He didn't know what in the world he was thinking when he thought he could handle this job on his own.

"Listen, Cameron Tan." Addressing him by his full name was Jill's way of saying these orders were not up for debate. "The extraction team that was supposed to meet you and the agent was forced to withdraw. However, they buried a CRRC in the sand just in case you arrived late. You know what that is, right?"

"Of course I do, Mom," he replied.

"Tao, what is—?"

A combat rubber reconnaissance craft. Basically, they buried a raft for us.

"Good, it's on the western tip of Alonaki Fanariou beach. Dig it up and head straight west to Italy. Find the nearest IXTF or Prophus command group. You are under strict orders to avoid all hot zones. Your package is more important. Do you understand?"

"Yes, Keeper."

"Good. Now…" Cameron could hear her take a deep breath. "How are you? Are you all right?"

Ask her for a status with the Genjix. How are the Prophus and IXTF responding?

"I'm fine, mom. The government here has completely locked down Internet and phone access. What's going on with the rest of the world?"

The news was as bad as he feared. At exactly 2300 Greenwich Mean Time, an all-out attack from the Genjix countries hit Poland, the eastern-most Prophus-allied country in Europe. Fortunately, between Nazar's warning and early detection systems, the Prophus-allied countries were able to send out an alert and weren't completely blindsided.

Midnight in France. Lucia's birthday had multiple meanings. It also indicated when the attack was to commence globally.

The Genjix had also hit South Africa, Canada, Australia, India and South Korea. Taiwan, Finland, Peru, Thailand and several other smaller countries and territories had already fallen. Like Greece, the governments of Tanzania, Colombia and Egypt had declared alliance with the Genjix. Canada, Venezuela and Greece were rapidly falling into civil war.

"I mean, do you believe that?" Jill sighed. She sounded tired. "Quebec is allying with the Genjix. I don't even know where to start with that."

Even Tao seemed to have one of his extraordinarily rare speechless moments. *Oh. My. This...this is much worse than I could possibly imagine.*

"What about dad?" Cameron asked.

"Your father is with Kallis, the IXTF chief, telling the Security Council to get off their collective asses."

The door behind him banged open, and Cameron jumped out of the bench with a start. Yang, wheezing and out of breath, staggered up to him. "I was looking all over for you. You said you were going to go sleep."

Cameron covered the phone with his palm and silently mouthed a "what?" to Yang.

"Wait, how is your phone working?" Yang frowned.

"Never mind," Cameron replied. "What do you need?"

"Someone is coming! Two cars heading up the path."

We are in a pretty remote area. It has to be the Genjix. How did they find us?

Cameron put the phone back next to his ear. "Mom, I have to go!"

"Wait, Cameron, I love—"

Cameron didn't hear the rest of her words. He didn't need to. He had known that his entire life.

Found

Unmarked, *but definitely a model used by the Hellenic police.*

Cameron wished he had binoculars, but he didn't need them as long as he had Tao. His Quasing was able to maximize the use of all of a human's abilities, including sight. Now, as he watched the two cars rumble up the windy path, he couldn't decide what to do next.

"Can it be a coincidence?" Seth asked. "With the chaos going on in the cities, they could just be rangers checking up on rural residences."

Nazar, standing next to Cameron peering through the window, drew his pistol and checked his magazine. "Can't risk it. No other choice."

Cameron was inclined to agree and drew his as well. He only had six rounds left, but that would be enough.

Yang, standing off to the side, stared at the guns. "Wait, these are police. Maybe they're just doing their jobs. Let me talk to them."

"No way." Cameron shook his head. "Nazar, I want you upstairs near the far window, where it's safe. I'll take the close one down here so we can catch them in a crossfire. The rest of you head out to the back and hide in the temple."

"What if they get inside?" Nazar asked. "I'll be trapped up there."

"If they do, I'm dead and I guess one of you gets promoted to a host. Congratulations."

"What if I don't want him?" Emily said.

"I don't want him either," Seth added.

Well I feel loved.

Nazar patted Cameron on the back with his bad hand. "How about neither of us die today?"

Yang shook his head. "Ambushing the police is wrong. They probably just found the truck on the side of the road and were checking to see if anyone needed help. We should to talk to them first."

"This is ridiculous," Cameron pressed. "You can't even speak the language."

Seth stepped forward. "I can. Kind of at least."

"Are you kidding?" Cameron sputtered.

"Yang's right," Seth said. "One of the things my parents had always taught me about the Prophus is that they value human life and that we treat them as equals. If we just open fire on these possibly innocent people, then that's murder. We can't shoot first and ask questions later."

Well, maybe not technically equals, but I see his point. Sometimes being safe is not worth the price of being righteous. They could be completely innocent Hellenic police following up on a truck on the side of the road, but I highly doubt it. Whoever goes to meet them will be out in the open and dangerously exposed. You will also lose the element of surprise.

"Yang, why don't you hide with the others and let Seth handle it then," Cameron said. "No need to risk both of you."

Yang shook his head. "No, this is my idea. I'm not going to hide and let Seth take all the risks. Besides, two kids who got lost hiking in the mountains look a lot less suspicious than one wandering by himself."

"What if they throw you in jail?" asked Negin.

Yang smiled bravely. "Once they find out who my family is, I'll get a free ride home. Trust me, I'll be fine. I'm worth a lot more unharmed. The worst that could happen is they send me home flying coach."

"What if they fly you home first class and throw Seth in jail?" asked Emily.

Yang shrugged at Seth. "I'll tell them he works for me. It's not uncommon for wealthy kids to put their friends on their payroll to keep them company. He'll be under my protection."

They had a point. There was a big difference between fighting Genjix and fighting local law enforcement. If Yang spoke with them first, this could resolve peacefully. Perhaps bloodshed could be avoided. Besides, if anyone had a free get-out-of-jail card, it was the son of Chinese millionaire industrialists.

"Fine, you guys," Cameron said, throwing his hands up in frustration. "If it's anything other than a random check, I want you to drop to the ground and lay flat. Do nothing. Just lie still and pretend you're dead."

"Don't have to worry about me. I'm sure I'll just faint anyway," Yang replied. He turned to Seth. "You have your passport on you? Let's get our alibis straight."

Cameron sent the rest to the temple and told them not to come back until he retrieved them. He exchanged some last-minute instructions with Nazar, and then positioned himself next to the window. By now, the cars had pulled up to the front yard. He counted eight people total, four uniformed, two in suits, and two in fatigues. The suits concerned Cameron more than the two military men.

That is a lot of bodies for a house call.

Yang and Seth, trying their best not to look nervous, waited at the end of the driveway. The four officers got out of the car and stayed in front instead of surrounding them. Their hands were relaxed at their sides. Yang and Seth handed them their passports and exchanged a few words. A couple of the officers laughed. They appeared to be able to understand what Seth was saying and the conversation seemed friendly. These were all positive signs. For a second, Cameron thought Yang was going to pull it off.

The men in suits were speaking in the back. The two in fatigues were wandering to the sides, eyes scanning the perimeter. They were definitely looking for something. Then, one of the suits took something out of a briefcase and held it in the air.

Penetra scanner!

No sooner did Tao say that, one of the suits pointed the Quasing detection device directly at Cameron's location and yelled something in Russian. Everything happened in an instant. The officer closest to Yang tackled him to the ground. Everyone else pulled out their guns. Seth turned back toward the house. A loud crack of a gunshot echoed in the air, and then he fell.

Cameron screamed and opened fire, hitting one of the officers before being forced to pull back behind cover. The concrete walls of the house began spitting fragments as a barrage of bullets shot through the open window and bit into the wall just over his head. He crawled to the next window, exhaled, and then spun into it, taking out another of the officers with two shots.

By now, the remaining officers had retreated behind their vehicles. The military guys charged forward from the sides, and one of the suits advanced on the front door. Cameron lost sight of the other.

The remaining two officers shot at the house, but not at Cameron. He heard return gunfire coming from upstairs and hoped Nazar played it safe. He was the vital asset, after all. Cameron peered through the other window at an angle and hit one of the military guys at the far side. The shot to the chest didn't seem to make it through his body armor. The second to the neck did the trick, though.

The front door of the house crashed open as one of the suits charged in. The guy swung to his right and fired, bullets kicking the ground where Cameron had been crouched moments before. Cameron dove to the side and scrambled to the back room.

One bullet left. Conserve if you can.

He crept to the corner between the two doors and listened for footsteps. The suit would either follow him from the front room on his right or enter through the hallway on his left. If he went up the stairs, Cameron would hear the steps.

A scream came from the backyard, and then he heard wood creak. Cameron hesitated.

The one going up the stairs will get the jump on Nazar.

"Damn it." Cameron turned into the hallway and saw legs between the gaps of the steps. He took a breath, aimed, and struck the guy in the shin. The man in the suit screamed and tumbled down the stairs. Cameron took off through the house and out to the backyard. He saw the other suit, pistol raised, approaching the temple.

Right handed. Weight on front leg. Thirty meter distance. That is a lot of ground.

The suit spun and opened fire. Eyes focused on the man's eyes, Cameron danced to his left and charged, juking from side to side. Bullets zinged past, just missing him by inches. He closed the distance and slid, kicking at the suit's ankles. He managed to only graze the man, who stumbled, but stayed on his feet.

Cameron shot in again, trapping the man's forearm and then with a twist and a kick, flipped him onto his stomach to the ground. Cameron plucked the pistol out of the guy's hands, and then fired twice at close range.

Emily popped her head out from the dark interior of the temple. "Thank God. Is everything all right?"

Well done. Hurry back to the front and check on Nazar.

"Just stay put," he yelled, checking the magazine in his newly-acquired pistol and then charging back to the house.

By the time he got back to the front of the house, everything was quiet. That could mean something good or something very, very bad. The man in the suit he had shot lay at the base of the stairs. He was clawing for the pistol he dropped halfway up the steps. Cameron dragged him back down to the floor by the collar and pocketed the pistol.

I have some questions for this one. Check the rest of the grounds first.

Cameron moved up next to the front door and leaned out the doorway. At first, he saw nothing, and then he saw Yang kneeling over Seth, who still lay face down on the ground.

"Oh no, oh no."

Wait!

Cameron threw caution to the wind and rushed outside. He already knew his friend was dead as soon as he started running. Yang looked up at him as he approached, tears streaming down his face. He fell to his knees and slowly rolled Seth onto his back. Seth's eyes were open, and he was staring off into nothing. Cameron put a hand to his mouth and a sob escaped his lips. His body shook his hand closed his friend's eyes.

Listen to me. You have to secure the area. Grieve for Seth later. Damn it, listen! If some of them are still alive, they could hurt your other friends.

That snapped Cameron out of it. He found the bodies of the four police officers, one of the military men where he had shot him, and the other closer to the house. He looked up at the window where Nazar was positioned. There was no one there.

Check on your people's wellbeing.

Cameron ran back into the house and bounded up the stairs. He found Nazar sitting on the ground, slumped against the wall. He was sweating and breathing heavily as he pressed a hand against his left arm.

Nazar waved. "At least they only hit my ugly arm, right? Thing couldn't be anymore useless anyway."

"Are you all right?" Cameron asked.

"Lucky shot, but I took care of those bastards. Are the kids all right?"

Cameron shook his head. "Seth…"

Nazar nodded. "I saw."

Cameron checked the wound. "Bullet went clean through." He grabbed a blanket from the bed and tore it into a long strip. He wrapped the wound as best he could and helped Nazar up.

"I'll be fine, boy," Nazar said, waving him off.

There was another gunshot from below. Cameron nearly dropped Nazar as he raced back down. Did he miss someone? He stopped halfway down the stairs and gaped as Yang stood over the man in the suit with a pistol in his hand.

Yang looked up at Cameron. "He was the one who shot Seth."

Damn it. I wanted to question him.

Cameron went down to the base of the stairs and took the gun from his friend's hands. "This isn't who you are, Yang."

"He shot Seth." Yang held up his blood-soaked hands. "He died in my arms." Cameron felt the tears well up in his eyes again. He hugged his shaking friend and led him away from the body. Cameron took him outside and sat him down in the chair. Yang broke down and began to sob.

Nazar came down a moment later. He checked the body for identification and pocketed the spare magazines. "I'll get the others. We should think about getting as far away from this place as possible."

He is right. You have nine bodies, including military and police, and most likely Genjix operatives. Pull yourself together and take care of those who are still alive. Also, you have a very serious problem on your hands.

"What's that, Tao?"

This is my fault. I should have seen it earlier. Tread very carefully from this point on, Cameron, but we have a traitor in our midst.

The Final Leg

They buried Seth in a shallow grave near the temple. It had to be shallow, since they had to use the broken and dull tools that hadn't been scavenged from the house in decades of disuse. Everyone pitched in. The sounds of their crying filled the air. Emily was particularly devastated and inconsolable, staying by the grave until the very last second. She had known Seth since they were kids.

"We have to go," Cameron said, gently.

"We can't leave him here," she sobbed. "I promised his mum I'd take care of him…"

"We'll come back and bring him home one day." He meant it too. Seth deserved more than this.

They procured one of the cars and squeezed everyone in. Cameron looked back at the villa one last time as they pulled away. It was a stab to the heart, and it hurt so terribly he wanted to weep. This was as personal of a failure as he had ever experienced.

You did your best, Cameron. The responsibility is yours, but you cannot allow yourself to get weighed down by every tragedy.

"Of course I can, Tao. It's my fault."

This is war, son. It does not matter who is at fault.

The drive west down route E952 was unbearably quiet. No one spoke or made a noise during the entire trip, save for an occasional groan of discomfort from Nazar as he shifted in the front seat next to him. Cameron would occasionally look in the rear view mirror and see Emily and Negin, eyes red and wet, holding each other tightly.

Cameron was thankful for this quiet on the outside, because it was all he could do to handle the storm raging inside his head. At this moment, he was having a full-blown meltdown with Tao, arguing over whether there was actually a traitor in the group.

"That's crazy. If I had to suspect anyone, I would have thought it'd be Chris, but he left us back in Athens."

Think about it. First, we get hit at Ira's Hearth, and now these men find us at the villa. They were also informed enough to bring a Penetra scanner. This is no coincidence.

"How could you think that? Look at what happened to Seth. Look at the tears in everyone's eyes!" Cameron knew he was grasping at straws but he couldn't help it. They were his friends, and good friends at that. He had spent an entire summer with them.

You cannot judge innocence this way. Perhaps the traitor did not mean for Seth to die. Maybe he is just a Genjix sympathizer trying to earn favor.

"But why? The Prophus ran a background check on everyone before I enrolled. None of these are Genjix."

You know how easily background checks can be washed. Look, it is safe to say that Emily and Seth are not Genjix. However, both Negin and Yang are from Genjix-controlled countries, and Surrett is from a border country that will be one of the most hotly contested in the war. Even if they are not Genjix, the three of them have reason to be.

"I don't buy it. Look at the things we've been through. There were dozens of other opportunities for them to capture us. Yang even shot one of them."

Yang is my main suspect. Think about it. He was the one who volunteered to speak with the Genjix at the front of the house instead of letting us ambush them. He was the one who killed the remaining

Genjix, who may have had the answers to our questions. And with his powerful family in China, we know he must have direct dealings with the Genjix in one form or another. It may have been his plan all along to get caught at the front of the house in order to extract himself from danger.

Cameron couldn't help but stare through the rear-view mirror at Yang sitting at the window seat, looking outside. He wasn't crying anymore, but his face was still red. He wiped his face as he held onto that damn viola of his. As if somehow knowing he was being watched, Yang turned and looked at Cameron, and nodded. Cameron looked away.

Tao's words began to sink in, and they hurt him. Badly.

You may have to consider the possibility that they knew who you were all along, that it was their job to get close to you.

There it was. It was a thought in the back of Cameron's mind that was poking into his brain like sharp needles. If what Tao said was true, then the friendships he had made this summer were fake. Someone was using him to get to Tao and his mom.

I doubt that, though. The Genjix would never pass up the opportunity to capture me or the Keeper's son.

Their argument continued until they reached Loutsa on the western edge of Greece. Alonaki beach was just a few more kilometers past the resort town. However, they had been driving for over ten hours and he was exhausted. He did not relish digging up the raft in the middle of the night and trying to navigate the Ionian Sea tired, hungry and without any supplies or food.

There was also the matter of the possible spy. If what Tao said was true, while they were digging up the raft would be the perfect time to set up an ambush. They would be exhausted from the work, and their backs would be to the sea, cutting off their escape routes. If they managed to escape on the raft, the CRRC, composed entirely of rubber, would be susceptible to small arms fire. No, Cameron and Tao had to figure out a way to escape without the potential traitor selling them out.

You must find out who this traitor is and make sure they are not on the raft with us.

Problems upon problems. Just when it seemed like they were so close. "Can we worry about that once we actually escape the country?"

Our problem will not disappear even if we manage to escape Greece. From what Jill said, Italy is in chaos at the moment. The Genjix can follow us into Italy as long as the traitor is with us. Even if you make it there, you will still be in great danger.

The group abandoned the stolen car half a kilometer outside of Loutsa and walked the rest of the way into town. He was surprised that the town did not seem affected by the coup, at least not yet. He had to remind himself it had only been a day. It felt like he'd been on the run for weeks now.

They pooled their money together and stopped by a local convenience store to pick up supplies. They had enough left over to pay for one night's stay at a small rundown motel off the main strip of town. Cameron made sure that the room they rented was on the second floor, with the front door opening to a balcony hallway that overlooked the woods.

With their remaining funds, they splurged on a group dinner at a local gyro restaurant. They technically didn't have enough money to cover the entire meal, but they bartered Yang's watch to cover the difference. Cameron had stressed to everyone how important it was not to use credit cards. Tao wanted to go one step further and search everyone for anything suspicious. However, Cameron wasn't ready to be so draconian.

Those was the most expensive gyros we have ever had.

"No kidding. I hope that wasn't an expensive watch."

I am pretty sure it was. Did you see the look on Yang's face?

Dinner, like the drive, was muted. Seth's death was still fresh on everyone's mind, and the fact that they were eating gyros only depressed Cameron even more. He never did get to have that last meal with everyone at that joint near their dorms. He decided at that time to break the silence and enact the secret plan. He made a big show of receiving a call on his phone. He got up from the table and walked out the restaurant, and then returned five minutes later.

"Okay guys, we finally got a spot of luck." Cameron tried his best to sound thrilled. "Change of plans. We're in the clear."

Again, theater major. You need some training, or at least an elective.

"About time something went our way," Negin smiled.

Cameron toned down his cheerfulness. "I got in contact with the Prophus. They've prioritized our escape and are sending a team to extract us from the city and fly us to safety."

Both Surrett and Negin cheered. Nazar and Emily looked puzzled. Yang looked pissed.

"What happened to digging up the raft?" Nazar asked.

Cameron shrugged. "We don't need it anymore. It's first class all the way out of Greece."

Yang scowled and pointed at the bags of stuff they had purchased an hour before. "We just bought three shovels, water-proof bags, binoculars, a bunch of headlamps, and thirty bottles of water!"

"So?"

"So," Yang emphasized the word. "If we're just getting air-lifted out, why did we buy all that? We could have used that money to pay for dinner, and then I wouldn't have had to pawn a ten thousand dollar watch for a bunch of strips of lamb."

Cameron was taken aback. "That was a ten thousand dollar watch? Shoot, we should have gotten a round of drinks with our meal."

"You owe me a new watch, Cameron!"

"How about I get us to safety instead? Unfortunately, I got the good news after we bought all that stuff. Sorry about your watch." Cameron really wasn't. He had a sinking feeling Tao was right about their traitor.

"So when are they coming?" Surrett asked. "Where are they picking us up?"

"They know where we're staying," Cameron replied. "Someone will knock on the room door between three and five in the morning, so pack right when we get back to the motel and be ready to go."

"Tonight?" Negin put her hand over his and shook him with excitement. She then reached to her other side and hugged Emily.

Cameron's grin extended from ear to ear and his cheeks flushed. "I told you I'd take care of you."

Easy there. You are trying too hard.

The only person who didn't look happy was Yang, who continued to stare at the blank space on his wrist where the watch used to be. "My grandmother gave me that," he grumbled.

Once the commotion settled down, Cameron checked the time, and then stood up. "All right, I'm freaking exhausted. Everyone turn in early. It's still going to be another long night so get some rest."

In Their Midst

The Genjix came at two in the morning. There were somewhere between eight and twelve total, a line of silhouettes moving with military precision across the second-floor balcony hallway toward their room. A man was stationed at the bottom of the stairwell, another manned the end of the driveway, and a few more dotted the perimeter. Four of the Genjix huddled next to the door, one of them kicked it open, and they all rushed inside.

Hidden in the woods approximately three hundred meters away, safely out of range of the Quasing-tracking Penetra scanners, Cameron watched the action unfold. The trap he and Tao had devised to confirm if they had a traitor in the group worked perfectly. He felt his heart turn to stone even as it dropped to the ground and shattered. The enemy knew exactly where to go, what exits to cover, and at what time to raid the motel room. He turned to the group huddled in the thickets behind him. "Get moving. I'll meet you as soon as I can."

Nazar nodded. "Let's go."

Negin looked scared and confused. "I don't understand what just happened. Where are you going, Cameron?"

Cameron turned his back to her. "Move. Now." He grabbed Emily's arm as she passed. "Don't let any of them out of your sight, especially Yang. I don't know how this person is getting in touch with the Genjix, but watch them like a hawk."

She nodded, her face grim. "Take care of yourself. When can you meet up with us?"

"Once I'm sure I'm not being followed or tracked by a Penetra scanner."

One good piece of intel is that the Genjix do not have a tracking beacon on us. If they had, they would have come directly to this spot. I had feared the traitor would have it hidden on his person somewhere.

"Like in a viola case?"

Sounds as good a place to hide a bug as any.

Cameron spent the next twenty minutes tracking the people tracking him, staying far enough out of the Penetra scanner's range, but close enough to know where they were headed. It was one of the first rules of being the hunted: tail the hunter.

By now, they must have realized that the intel they had received from the traitor was bad, and were either hoping to pick up his signal or wait for the traitor to contact them again. They stayed around the motel for another fifteen minutes before heading south to Vrachos Beach, away from Alonaki where the CRRC was buried. He stayed with them for twenty more minutes before breaking off.

You are far enough away. Get your people and get out of this country.

Cameron's emotions were a bubbling cauldron of conflicted and unfocused anger as he made his way north to his friends. The truth hurt; it hurt badly. Outside of Emily, the three survivors still with him were his closest friends this summer. One of them was a Genjix, or at least was actively working with the Genjix. That traitor had led to Seth's death. The very thought made him want to throw up.

"I'm such an idiot, Tao. First Alex, and now these guys."

This is a sad and all-too-common occurrence in our line of work. You must harden your soul, because this will happen again. Edward

Blair, my host before Roen, was betrayed by his partner. In the future, people must not earn your friendship and trust so easily.

Cameron hated that idea, but he had been burned far too many times in his young life. This was the last time. It had to be. His anguish and pain turned into rage when he reached the beach. The fact that he wasn't sure who it was just made things worse. He didn't know at whom he should direct his wrath.

Nazar, standing on top of a small dune at the edge of the rock outcropping, saw him first. Yang, Surrett and Negin, were waist-deep digging a pit in the soft sand with the shovels they had purchased at the convenience store. By now, they had unearthed most of the rubber craft.

"Cameron!" Negin said, trying to climb out of the hole to greet him.

"Stay there. Keep working." He spoke more harshly than he had intended, but he was having trouble not lashing out at one of them. He immediately felt bad for the hurt look on her face. "Let's just focus on getting the work done." He stood next Nazar and watched the progress below. "How goes it?"

"We should be able to start inflating the craft soon." He held up his mangled left arm. "It's the one perk for having this. I get to skip all the menial labor."

Cameron leaned in closer and whispered. "Any suspicious activity?"

Nazar shook his head. I've been keeping careful watch on our friends. Whoever it is, he hasn't had a chance to contact the Genjix."

"Where's Emily?"

"We didn't need four bodies to dig since we only have three shovels and two headlamps." He pointed at small piece of land sticking out into the water. "I sent her over there. There's a high vantage point that gives eyes on a good part of the beach as well as the road leading up here from Loutsa. I can call her back anytime with two blinks of a flashlight."

"Good."

By now, the three students were struggling to lift the raft out of the hole. Cameron jumped in to help push the large black rubber cube to the surface. They unrolled it and after some puzzling together, began to attach the motor to the back of the craft. Emily appeared a few minutes later, just as they were about to start inflating it.

"There are people coming up along the beach," she panted in between breaths. "I can't tell how many."

Damn it. How did they find us?

"Do they know we're here?" Cameron asked. "How far away are they?"

She shook her head. "I don't think so. They can't be more than half a kilometer away. I think they're just moving up along the beach. I couldn't quite tell through my binoculars. It's too dark. I thought I saw a Penetra scanner."

The craft will need about ten minutes to inflate and be ready to deploy. Fifteen optimally.

That was an eternity. Not to mention that the noise the inflater was going to make would be a dead giveaway. Cameron drew his pistol. "I'm going to buy us some time. Keep working and get it into the water. If I'm not back in fifteen minutes, leave without me. If you see them approaching, leave without me."

Emily gasped. "No, you can't."

Nazar nodded. "Don't force our hand, Cameron. Until the Eternal Sea."

Cameron paused and looked back. "If I don't make it, tell my parents...tell them sorry, and that I tried my best."

Yang made a face. "Are you crazy? You can't go up against an army of guys by yourself. Wait, Cameron, let me help."

"You stay with the others!" Cameron hissed. "Don't you dare follow me."

He began sprinting south down the beach.

"You're not seriously going to let him go by himself, are you?" he heard Yang say to the others.

Cameron crashed through the trees, abandoning all attempts at stealth. He needed to put as much distance between the Genjix and his friends as possible. Besides, if they did have a Penetra scanner with them, it was useless trying to be sneaky.

You have two full magazines, twenty rounds. Do not stay put for more than one grouping. If you need to waste bullets, waste them taking out the one with the scanner. You may have a fighting chance then.

Cameron reached the top of a small crest near the edge of the water and saw the group moving up along the beach.

"Wow that is a lot of bodies."

Cameron, it is too many. You have little to no chance of surviving that fight.

"Well, maybe I can buy enough time for Nazar and those guys to escape. That'd be worth my life, right?"

Honestly, no. If there is one thing I learned from you and Roen, it is that you are worth more to me than what is on that air drive. I would order you to abort this mission and save yourself if I thought you would listen.

"You're right about that, Tao."

About what?

"I'm not going to listen."

There. See that. One of them near the back just pointed in our direction. They know you are here. That guy just marked himself as the one with the Penetra scanner.

Cameron aimed his sights at the man holding the Penetra scanner and trailed his movements. The Genjix were still over a hundred meters away. Even from his higher vantage point, it was an impossible shot. He'd have to wait until they closed the distance. However, if he waited too long, they would have him pinned with his back to the sea. He began to move inland to give himself more room to maneuver.

No, stay put. They have slowed their advance. They think they are getting the jump on you. Use this to your advantage. Hold your shot. Hold...

Cameron relaxed, emptied his mind, and let go. He inhaled, exhaled, and found calm in the chaos. Tao's voice echoed through his body, his words seemed to merge with Cameron's thoughts. He felt himself detach from his body, even while his vision sharpened and hands steadied. He felt more in control than ever, even with Tao's subtle touch directing his aim.

Fire.

Cameron pulled the trigger before Tao even finished the word. He was rewarded with the silhouette of his target falling from his sights. Immediately, the ground around him began to pop with bullets. He pulled back and disappeared into dark forest. In a way, this situation felt familiar. When he was a teenager, one of his fondest memories was Jill's early-morning games of tag in the forest. Where Tao taught Cameron tactics and Roen taught him how to fight, Jill taught him guile.

Tao began translating everything the Genjix agents were shouting in Russian. "Spread out and move in twos. Keep line of sight. Yuryev, find where Pavel fell and get that scanner. Who has the flame thrower?"

Cameron made short work of the first two Genjix who crossed his path. He let the first one slip past him and jumped on the second. A quick body lock and snap of the neck, and the man was dead. Then, still holding the body as a shield, he turned toward the first, who managed to shoot two rounds into his friend. Cameron returned fire, taking him down with three shots, then disappeared back into the shadows.

The next two he got the drop on, climbing up a tree branch, moving around the trunk to the other side, and dropping down from above them. His aim was a little off, and he crashed onto the ground behind his intended target. Fortunately, his flailing arms struck the guy in the side of the head, and they both went down. Cameron rolled to his side, feeling dirt kick up where he had been a split second earlier.

To your left, near 10:30.

Cameron shot blind, and his faith in Tao was rewarded with a groan and a body falling forward. He scrambled to his feet and plugged two slugs into the guy next to him, then one more down into the guy he had hit earlier. He came up lame and grimaced as he retreated into cover. The ground was slanted and uneven with tree roots and loose dirt, and his ankle hadn't liked that landing.

Shake it off. Three rounds left in the magazine.

"Four down, like five or ten to go."

By now, the Genjix knew they had their hands full and were reorganizing, consolidating their ranks and shifting their flank to the right. Cameron crouched behind a thick tree and scanned his surroundings. He had less than fifteen meters to play with before hitting the water, and about twenty of open space before they had him boxed in.

"I'm not liking this situation much."

I'm not, either. To your right. One in sight by himself. Go low and quiet.

Cameron dove from his position, grabbed the guy around the waist, spun, and threw him on the ground. Kneeling on top, he struck the man in the temple once and was about to deliver the killing blow when pain exploded through his body, first in his shoulder, and then in his hip. He fell onto his back and instinctively opened fired, taking out at least one of the guys who had shot him.

"We got him," one of them shouted. "Vadim, bring the flamethrower. Don't kill the boy until he is in position to fry the Holy One."

Cameron blocked the kick of the first Genjix who jumped on top of him, and shot two rounds into the man's body at close range. He looked to his other side at two more charging in. He shot the first one in the chest, but his next three trigger pulls were empty clicks.

A kick in the arm knocked the pistol out of his hand. Something hard struck him in the side of the face. Another kick to the gut bent him over into a fetal position. He tried to cover the blows raining down on him, blocking another kick to his face, but taking a hard shot in the back made him arch backward.

Sweep out and crawl to your right. There's two more coming behind you. Let me take control.

However, it was too late. Cameron couldn't quite grasp the balance of calmness and clarity needed for Tao to take control through all this pain. Someone punched him so hard he momentarily blacked out. Stunned and in shock, he watched the world sideways as one of the Genjix calmly strolled toward him with a hand-held flamethrower.

Panic grabbed ahold of Cameron and he felt a momentary burst of energy. He glanced through the trees at the sea just a few meters away. He might not survive this fight, but if he could make it close enough to open water, maybe Tao could escape and find another host. That would be victory enough. If he bought enough time for the others to escape, that would be gravy on top of everything else.

Cameron reached out with one hand and clawed the dirt, pulling himself a few centimeters toward the sea. He reached out with his other, and then one of the Genjix stepped on it, and he felt the bones in his hand crack. Cameron screamed.

"Where do you think you're going, betrayer?" This time, the Genjix spoke in English.

"Vadim, come here," another Genjix said. "Everyone else step back. "Once I shoot him in the head, Vadim fries the Holy One."

Cameron felt cold metal pressed against the back of his head. He closed his eyes, and thought about his mom and dad, and how much pain they would be in when they found out he had died. He thought about Tao, and how sad it was for such an eternally old and wise being to die today. Cameron felt so sorry, not just for Tao and his parents, but to Seth and Emily and Nazar. He had let everyone down.

That is not true, Cameron. You have been the joy of my existence. Find peace, my son. Until the Eternal—

Half a dozen loud pops punctured the air. A body fell on top of him, and then he heard yelling, and strangely a high-pitched, squeaky war cry. The roar continued for several seconds until it cut off as quickly as it came.

Gritting his teeth, Cameron rolled over and pushed the body off of him. He looked around and saw several more Genjix laying on the ground. Some were no longer moving; others were groaning and struggling to get up. Further away, a Genjix with his back to him was cautiously walking toward something near the edge of the ridge line.

Then Cameron saw him, Yang Shi, with his glasses crooked on his face, slumped against a tree. There was blood all over his chest, and his head was tilted to the side. His body spasmed and he coughed. He was still alive.

Ignoring the excruciating pain coursing through his body, Cameron struggled to his feet and half-ran, half-hopped toward the Yang. He struck the back of the head of a Genjix who was trying to stand, and grabbed his gun. Cameron grimaced again as his broken left hand tried to clasp the pistol. He raised it and fired, striking the stalking Genjix in the back.

To your right!

Cameron swung around and shot another Genjix rising to his feet. He scanned the area around him and plugged every remaining body with a slug to make sure they were all dead. He counted over thirteen bodies in all.

That should be all of them.

The pistol fell from Cameron's hand as he hopped on his one good foot toward Yang. His friend looked up at him, and blinked. "I didn't think…it was a fair fight, so…I came to even the odds, Cameron." He coughed again and blood dribbled from his lips.

"You were supposed to stay with the others," Cameron choked.

"I need to ask you…for a favor, Cameron Sun," Yang said.

"It's Tan, Yang. My name is Cameron Tan. Ask me for anything."

"Can you bring my viola back to my parents? I…I think my little sister will want it, even if she always preferred the violin." His head lolled to the center, and Yang Shi died.

Cameron closed Yang's eyes. Overcome by grief, he hugged the body of the friend who had saved both him and Tao. He began to cry. How could he be so wrong about everything, about everyone?

"I turned on him so easily."

I misjudged him as well. I thought he was guilty too. I am sorry.
The minutes passed. Cameron didn't know how long he stayed there. He didn't care. This man had saved his life. He deserved better than to be left here among his killers.

Cameron, I know you do not want to hear this but we have to go. If Yang is not the traitor, then it is one of the others. We cannot leave Nazar and Emily by themselves. The Genjix will find them unless you guide them to safety. We have to go. Cameron!

The thought of losing Emily brought Cameron back. He nodded, whispered one more thank-you to Yang, and promised to fulfill that final request. Ignoring the pain everywhere in his body, Cameron struggled to his feet and hobbled back to the others.

Consequences

Cameron had half-expected the group to be gone by the time he returned to Alonaki beach. However, they were all still there and apparently waiting for him. The rubber craft was inflated, the motor was installed, and it was now sitting in the water. That made what he was about to do worse in many ways. He checked the time.

"It's been twenty minutes," he said. "You guys suck at telling time."

"Blame her." Nazar threw a thumb at Emily. "Girl wouldn't let me leave. Trust me, I tried."

Emily, who was standing at the back of the craft guarding the motor with her arms crossed, shook her head. "I lost one best friend already. I'm not losing another."

"Cameron," Negin said. "Did you see Yang? He went to go find you."

Fresh tears rolled off Cameron's eyes. He shook his head. "He's gone."

She began to cry and threw herself into his arms. Cameron hesitated and then embraced her.

"He grabbed Emily's gun when she put it down to help install the motor," Surrett said quietly. "We tried to tell him to stay. He wouldn't listen."

"He saved my life," Cameron replied. "He probably saved all our lives."

He looked over and saw Yang's viola case lying on its side. He let go of Negin and picked it up. He opened it slowly and carefully, and examined the instrument inside. His throat caught at the curve of the wood and the beauty of its shape. He strummed the strings and felt the viola vibrate as it came alive.

"So this is what all the fuss is about," he murmured.

It is beautiful.

Cameron closed the case and put it inside one of the waterproof packs. "I'm taking this back to his family." He stepped onto the raft and helped Nazar on board. When Negin reached her hand out to him for help getting on, Cameron drew his pistol and pointed it at her. Negin's eyes widened, and she stepped back with her hands raised.

"What are you doing, Cameron?" Emily gasped.

"Put that down," Nazar said.

Cameron moved the gun to point at Surrett. "One of you is a Genjix spy. You've been feeding them our locations, and you got Seth and Yang killed."

"How can you believe that?" said Negin.

"You're crazy, you know that?" said Surrett.

"I can't take any more chances," Cameron replied. His cheeks burned and his vision blurred. He could feel his arms shaking under the weight of the pistol. He must be weak after that harrowing fight, or perhaps it was something else. In any case, he knew he couldn't hold it up for much longer, not without breaking down entirely.

He turned his back to Negin and Surrett. "Get us out of here."

"Cameron..." Emily whispered. "Don't..."

"Now!"

"No!"

The look on her face cut deep into him. Cameron all of a sudden found that he had nowhere to look, so he just stared at the floor of the craft. "Get us moving. Please."

Nazar gently moved her to the side. "Let me."

"We're not…" her voice trailed off as Nazar spoke softly into her ear. "It'll be all right, girl. We need to go."

Cameron continued not to look at the friends he was abandoning. A part of him wanted to tell them how sorry he was for doing this, that he had no choice. He just couldn't risk being wrong again. He had done it far too many times, and there was too much at stake. What hurt the most was that even if he was right, and one of them was a Genjix spy, that would mean that the other one probably wasn't. That meant he was at best leaving someone innocent stranded.

Cameron didn't look back at the shore until they were past the break point. When he did, all he could see in the darkness was the sand and the waves and the trees behind them. Then he saw the two silhouettes standing alone on the beach, still in the same spot he had abandoned them, hoping that he would change his mind at the very last minute and come back.

Cameron took a deep breath and slowly let the air escape his lungs. The calming exercise did not work. The adrenaline drained from his body and then the dozen injuries he had sustained during the fight came rushing back.

He sat down next to Emily and spoke quietly. "The Genjix were able to follow us every step of the way. They would have kept hounding us until we got rid of the leak. I had no choice. You have to—"

Emily turned away from him and looked out to sea into the darkness.

The trip to safety was equally perilous and nerve wracking, if not outright dangerous. It took the three of them a day of being tossed around in the Ionian Sea before they reached Italy. The country was in complete chaos. It was the new front line for the battle for the Mediterranean. The Genjix forces had walked into most of the northern African countries hardly firing a shot. Egypt and Greece were now embroiled in civil war. Israel had completely closed its borders.

Cameron and the two survivors joined the throngs of humanity fleeing up the length of Italy, trying to escape the fighting. They moved from refugee camp to refugee camp, passing numerous checkpoints until they made contact with an IXTF unit who arranged for their transportation by train from Italy to Switzerland and then finally to Paris.

Once they reached Paris, Cameron was moved to a hospital where he stayed for a week so he could have his wounds dressed and the slugs in his body taken out. The wound in his hip had festered and had left him weakened and walking with a limp. Between that, the one in his shoulder, his two fractured ribs, and a punctured eardrum, Cameron had more than enough souvenirs to bring home. However, it wasn't what he had brought back with him that worried Tao.

Cameron left a part of himself back in Greece; he couldn't quite put his finger on what. He felt incomplete, as if part of his soul or whatever made up Cameron's being had broken into pieces. Seth and Yang's death and his decision to leave Negin and Surrett behind kept him up for hours every night. Once he would fall asleep, they haunted his dreams. He often woke screaming their names, crying sorry to whoever was close by. He would replay everything over and over both when he was awake and when he was asleep. No matter what, he couldn't let go, and he couldn't stop blaming himself.

He couldn't stop hating himself.

It wasn't until the fifth day at the hospital, staring out the window, that something strange happened. Cameron's hand took on a life of its own and slapped him. He saw the hand coming, moving from his side until it extended away from his body, and then moved toward his face, all completely out of his control. He frowned, confused. He wasn't sure if he should stop it until it connected with the right side of his face. He was so shocked he tipped over his chair and fell.

He stood up angrily. "Hey, what the hell? You hit me!"

I am tired of this. You did what you had to do. For the last time, this is not your fault. Own your decisions, and move on.

"You're abusing our symbiotic relationship, Tao."

And I am going to keep doing this until you snap out of it.

Rage came to Cameron easily, and he was about to scream at his Quasing when he noticed the patient next to him laughing uproariously. Cameron looked in the mirror at the angry red handprint on his face. He must have looked like an idiot smacking himself.

He couldn't help it. He began to chuckle. "Thanks Tao. I probably needed that."

Yes you did, son.

"I'm still going to get you back for it one day."

I eagerly await your revenge.

Cameron looked over at Emily sitting next to him staring out the window. She hadn't even noticed he fell. "Can you snap her out of it too?"

Emily wore the same haunted expression on her face as Cameron did, and even right next to him, she seemed a million miles away. He had tried to talk to her a few times after that night, but she hadn't responded. It hurt him that she blamed him for the decisions he was forced to make. He felt like she must hate him, yet she never left his side.

Give her time. She has been through a lot.

"So have all of us."

Yes, but you are a soldier. You understand that these hard choices must be made. She does not.

A somber Roen came later that day to discharge him. It had been months since Cameron had seen his father. Roen was a little grayer in the head, a little softer in the midsection, and dared Cameron say it, a little wiser in the face. That, or he just looked tired. Probably tired.

"Thank God you're all right," Roen said as he grabbed Cameron and pulled him into a tight embrace.

Cameron squeezed back until his hurt body ached. "I see the desk job is treating you well."

"That better be from Tao and not you," his father replied. I'm sorry I couldn't meet you earlier. The world is falling apart on me. Damn Canadians." Roen pulled back and looked him over. "Wow, you look worse than that time I dared you to catch a rooster."

"Yeah, well, you're a terrible father for letting me try, and I got these genes from you."

"I'm going to have some serious words with Tao tonight." Roen noticed Nazar standing behind Cameron for the first time. "Agent Sajjadi, I presume."

"Nazar got us here from Italy," Cameron said. I don't think we would have made it otherwise."

Nazar, the man Cameron had been assigned to save, had become their caretaker since they left Greece. He helped carry them during the long walks up Italy, protected them while at the refugee camps, and was the one who made contact with the IXTF.

Roen extended a hand. "You have my thanks, sir."

"Director," Nazar shook it. "It is an honor to meet Cameron Tan's father. You've raised a fine young man."

"He's all right," Roen grinned. "Just a little hard of hearing sometimes. I hear you have valuable information. It better be worth getting my son shot and beat up over."

Nazar patted his briefcase. "I need to see Command immediately."

Roen nodded. "We have a transport departing this afternoon. It'll take you and my son to Prophus Command in Greenland. I hope you packed your thermals."

"What about you, Dad?" Cameron asked.

Roen shook his head and pointed in a random direction. "The front line is that way. I'll be home in a few weeks."

East is the other direction.

Cameron let Roen know.

Roen scowled. "Both still smartasses, I see."

"Dad, if you're staying, I am as well. I want to fight."

His father's expression changed, and he stared Cameron down. "Son, grow up. You just fought through a terrible ordeal. I'm not sending you home because I want to keep you out of danger. I'm sending you home because I want you rested and recovered. It's going to be a long war, Cameron. I need you at full strength."

Roen is absolutely right. Wow, I cannot believe I just said that.

Cameron, who had spent the past three days preparing to argue with his father about sending him home, stopped. He nodded. "Okay, Dad."

"Besides," Roen said, "Your mother is going kill me if I don't lock you down and ship you to her fortress of solitude as soon as I get my paws on you."

"Sound like I'm going to jail."

"You're not passing Go or collecting two hundred dollars either," Roen replied cheerfully. "Come on, we have some time to kill before you head to the clink. Spend a few hours with your old man?"

Cameron looked over at Emily standing off to the side staring out the window. He didn't know what she was going to do next, but she was probably not coming to Greenland. This may be his last chance to say goodbye for a while.

"Sure, give me a second," Cameron said. "I'll be right there."

He walked to her and looked out the window. The hospital yard was a mess. A triage was set up in the center of the yard to take care of the incoming injured. Refugees flowed in by the hour. A food bank was handing out bottles of water. Next to it, the Red Cross was accepting blood donations. Everywhere he looked, he saw the best of humanity.

"I'm leaving for Greenland soon," he said.

Emily didn't reply at first, and then he felt the back of her hand brush against his, and then she clasped it. They stood there together, in silence, and continued to watch the activity outside.

"Did I ever tell you about my dad?" she finally said.

"No."

"He used to be an agent. I'm going to the States and see him. He got hurt on assignment a few years back. Never really recovered. His health has deteriorated recently. I was supposed to spend the summer with him instead of going to Greece. I ran away because I was too scared to deal with him dying." She paused. "He's a host."

"Oh? I didn't know that. You never talked about him."
Cameron's heart went out to her. There was something unique
and tragic for children of Prophus agents.

Emily nodded. "Io's been with my dad since he was young.
Dad always wanted one of his kids to be an agent so he could
pass Io along. That's why I ran from it, to be honest. After he got
injured, following in his footsteps was the last thing I wanted. But
now, I know what I want to do with my life. I want to fight. I want
to avenge Seth." She looked at him, and a small smile appeared.
"Maybe you could train me, give me some pointers."

"It would be my honor," he grinned back. "You know you'd
have to listen to whatever I say then."

She rolled her eyes. "Oh, never mind. It'll never work."

An IXTF agent interrupted them to let her know that her
transport to the airport had arrived. She threw her arms around
him. "Take care of yourself. You're my only best friend left." She
gave him one more squeeze and kissed him on the cheek, and
then she was gone.

"Tao, I didn't know her dad was a host. Do you know Io?"

Never heard of him, or at least he is not prominent.

"Really? I thought all you Quasing knew each other."

Hey Cameron, I know this one human. You must know him.

"Point made."

"Son, you hungry?" Roen said, coming up behind him. "I
found this pizza joint a few blocks away. It's French pizza—" he
made a face "—but French pizza's better than no pizza. Interested?"

Cameron smiled. He didn't love pizza as much as his father
did, but heck, who knew when the next time they were going to
have another meal together. "Sure, Dad, I'd love to. Lead the way."